"Mom, guess what?"

"What?"

"Deputy Alex is going to be your valentine!"

"What?" Several heads had turned at Emma's enthusiastic statement. No doubt there would be talk in the teacher's lounge later.

"I asked, and he said he doesn't have a valentine. And you don't have one either. So you can be each other's—it's perfect."

Emma's innocence made Cassie's heart squeeze. "Oh, honey, it's not quite that simple. Just because we're both single doesn't mean we're going to be valentines with each other."

Emma frowned. "Why not? Don't you like Deputy Alex?"

"Of course I do." More than she should. "But someday, when you're a grown-up, you'll understand that things like valentines are more complicated than just liking someone."

"I don't ever want to be a grown-up. It makes everything complicated."

No kidding, kid. No kidding.

* * *

PARADISE ANIMAL CLINIC:
Let the love—and fur-ever families—fly!

Dear Reader,

I have to admit, I almost couldn't wait to write this second Paradise Animal Clinic story and give Dr. Cassie Marshall her own happily-ever-after. Having been a single mother, I could really relate to her, and I know just how lonely it can be to be facing a future without your partner. And let's face it, trying to date when you are taking care of a kid isn't exactly easy. But I'm happy to say I eventually found my Prince Charming, and I thought Cassie deserved one, too—sexy sheriff's deputy Alex Santiago.

He's new in town, and the last thing he wants is to get involved with a single mother—or any woman, for that matter. His K-9 partner, Rex, is the only companion he needs. But Cassie's daughter, Emma, wants him to be her mother's valentine—and she isn't taking no for an answer!

I hope that all the single moms (and dads!) reading this remember that even if you have to take a few wrong turns before you get to Paradise, keep looking. It's out there.

Enjoy, and if you like this story, look for the other two books in my Paradise Animal Clinic series. In the meantime, I'd love to hear from you. You can find me at katiemeyerbooks.com, "like" me at facebook.com/katiemeyerbooks or follow me on Twitter, @ktgrok.

Happy reading!

Katie Meyer

A Valentine for
the Veterinarian

———

Katie Meyer

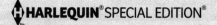
HARLEQUIN® SPECIAL EDITION®

Recycling programs
for this product may
not exist in your area

ISBN-13: 978-0-373-65942-5

A Valentine for the Veterinarian

Copyright © 2016 by Katie Meyer

This edition published by arrangement with Harlequin Books S.A.

For questions and comments about the quality of this book, please contact us at CustomerService@Harlequin.com.

HARLEQUIN®
™ www.Harlequin.com

Printed in U.S.A.

A12006 678305

Katie Meyer is a Florida native with a firm belief in happy endings. A former veterinary technician and dog trainer, she now spends her days homeschooling her children, writing and snuggling with her pets. Her guilty pleasures include good chocolate, *Downton Abbey* and cheap champagne. Preferably all at once. She looks to her parents' whirlwind romance and her own happy marriage for her romantic inspiration.

Books by Katie Meyer

Paradise Animal Clinic
The Puppy Proposal

Ean, for picking up the slack
and never complaining about it.

My mom and my son, Michael,
for babysitting the littles when I had a deadline
and needed some quiet.

My agent, Jill, for guiding me through the process.

And my editorial team,
especially Carly and Jennifer, for finding my
(numerous) mistakes and making me look good.

Chapter One

"Grace, you just saved my life. How can I ever repay you?"

The woman behind the counter rolled her eyes. "It's just coffee, Dr. Marshall, not the fountain of youth. If you leave a few coins in the tip jar, we'll call it even."

Cassie clutched the cardboard cup like a lifeline, inhaling the rich aroma. "I had an emergency call last night, ended up performing a C-section on a schnauzer at three a.m., and then was double-booked all day. So right now your caffeinated nectar is my only hope of making it through the meeting I'm going to." She paid for her coffee and took a cautious sip of the scalding brew. "You're my hero."

"That kind of flattery will get you the last cinnamon scone, if you want it."

"Have I ever turned down a free baked good?" Cassie

accepted the small white bag with the proffered pastry. "Thanks. This ought to keep me out of trouble until I can get some dinner."

"Speaking of trouble, here comes that new sheriff's deputy. I'd be willing to break a few rules if it would get him to notice me." Grace craned her neck to see more clearly out the curtained front window. "Don't you think he looks like a man who could handle my rebellious side?"

Cassie nearly spit out her coffee. If Grace Keville, sole proprietor of Sandcastle Bakery, had a rebellious side, she'd kept it well hidden. Even after a full day of baking and serving customers, she looked prim and proper in a crisp pastel blouse and tailored pants. From her lacy apron to her dainty bun, she was the epitome of order and discipline. Not to mention she was happily married and the mother of three. "You've never rebelled a day in your life."

Grace sniffed. "Maybe not, but that man makes me consider it. Hard."

Rebellion wasn't all it was cracked up to be. She'd been there, done that, and had considerably more than a T-shirt to show for it. She started to say as much, but stopped at the jingle of the door chimes behind her. Turning at the sound, she caught her breath at the sight of the intense man heading toward her with long, ground-eating strides.

No wonder Grace was infatuated. The man looked like he'd just stepped out of a Hollywood action movie rather than the quiet streets of Paradise, Florida. Thick, dark hair framed a chiseled face with just a hint of five-o'clock shadow. His eyes were the exact color of the espresso that scented the air, and reflected a focus that only men in law enforcement seemed to have. Even without the uniform she'd have known him for a cop. Sexy? Sure. But still a cop. And she'd had her fill of those.

"I'm here to pick up an order. Should be under Santiago."

Grace grabbed a large box from the top of a display case. "I've got it right here—an assortment of cookies, right?"

"That's right."

"What, no doughnuts?" Uh-oh, did she say that out loud?

He gave Cassie a long look before quirking up one side of his mouth. "Sorry to ruin the stereotype."

Grace glared at Cassie before attempting to smooth things over. "Deputy Santiago, I'm Grace. I'm the one you spoke to earlier on the phone. And this is Dr. Cassie Marshall, our resident veterinarian."

"Nice to meet you Grace, Dr. Marshall." He nodded at each in turn. "And off duty it's Alex, please." He smiled then, a real smile, and suddenly the room was too warm, too charged, for comfort. The man's smile was as lethal as the gun strapped to his hip—more potent than any Taser. Unsettled by her instant response, Cassie headed for the door. It wasn't like her to speak without thinking; she needed to get out of there before she embarrassed herself more than she already had.

"Let me get that." He reached the door before her, balancing the large cookie box in one hand and pulling open the door with the other. After her own snide comment, his politeness poked at her conscience.

"Sorry about the doughnut remark." There, her conscience was clear.

"I've heard worse." His expression hardened for a minute. "Don't worry about it."

She wouldn't; she had way too many other concerns to keep her occupied. Including the meeting she was going to be late to, if she didn't hurry. She nodded politely, then made a beeline for her hatchback. Setting the coffee in a cup holder, she cranked the engine and popped in a CD of popular love songs. She had less than ten minutes to put aside all the worries tumbling through her mind and get herself in a Valentine's Day kind of mood.

Alex watched the silver hatchback drive away, noting she kept the small vehicle well under the speed limit. Few people were gutsy enough to speed in front of a sheriff's deputy—but then again, the average person didn't spout off jokes about cops to his face, either. There had been resentment in those blue eyes. She'd disliked him—or at the least the uniform—on sight. He was used to gang members and drug dealers treating him that way, but a cute veterinarian? His gut said there was a story there, but he didn't need to make enemies in his new hometown. He had plenty of those back in Miami.

A loud bark snapped him out of his thoughts.

"I'm coming, boy."

At this point, he and his canine partner, Rex, were in the honeymoon period of their relationship, and the dog still got excited whenever he saw Alex return. Unlocking the car, he couldn't help but smile at the goofy expression on the German Shepherd's face. As a trained K-9, Rex was a criminal's worst nightmare, but to Alex he was the best part of his new job.

He'd never expected to live in a small-time town like Paradise, had never wanted to leave Miami. But when he testified against his partner, the department had turned against him. It didn't matter that Rick was guilty. Alex was the one they turned on.

He'd known that refusing to lie during his deposition meant saying goodbye to any chance of promotion. He could live with that. But when his name and address were leaked to a local gang he'd investigated, things changed.

Putting his own life at risk, that was just part of the job. Messing with his family, that was a different story. When his mom had come home one day to find threats spray-painted on her walls and her house trashed, he'd known they couldn't stay.

He could still see her standing in her ruined kitchen, white with fear. She'd aged ten years that humid night.

Guilt clawed at him. What kind of son was he to lead danger straight to her doorstep? He'd resigned the next day and spent his two-week notice hunting down the scum responsible.

Then he'd packed up and looked for a job, any job, where he could start fresh without a target on his back. When a position in the Palmetto County Sheriff's office became open, he'd jumped on it. Working with a K-9 unit was a dream come true; he'd often volunteered time with the unit back home. That experience, plus a stellar record, had landed him the position.

Having the dog around eased the loneliness of being in a new city and made the long night shifts required of newbies seem a little shorter.

Thankfully, his mom had been willing to move, too. She'd lived in Miami ever since she and his father emigrated from Puerto Rico. He'd worried she would fight against leaving, but she'd agreed almost immediately. Her lack of argument told him she was more rattled than she'd admitted.

And of course there was Jessica, his younger sister, to think about, too. She was away at college, but still lived at home on school holidays. His mom wouldn't want her in the line of fire, even if she wasn't afraid for herself.

Now Paradise was their home and all that was behind them.

As he drove down what passed for Main Street, he scanned the tidy storefronts, more out of habit than caution. The tiny island community couldn't be more different from fast-paced south Florida. Instead of high rises and strip malls, there were bungalows and family-owned shops. Miami had a vibrant, intoxicating culture, but working in law enforcement, he'd spent his hours in the less picturesque parts of town. Here, even the poorest neighborhoods were tidy and well kept.

Of course, nowhere was perfect, not even Paradise. Which was why he was missing valuable sleep in order to attend the Share the Love volunteer meeting. The sheriff's department was pairing with the county's department of children's services in a fundraiser, a Valentine's Day dance. The money raised would be used to start up a mentor program for at-risk kids. Some were in foster care and many had parents serving time or were in trouble themselves. When the department had posted a flier about the program, he'd been the first to volunteer. He'd been on the other side of that story; it was time to give back.

It took only a few minutes to cross the island and

reach the Sandpiper Inn, the venue for tonight's organizational meeting. The largest building on the island, it often was the site of community events.

Pulling into the gravel lot, he was surprised to see most of the parking spaces were full. Either the Sandpiper had a lot of midweek guests or the meeting was going to be larger than he'd expected.

He grabbed the box on the passenger seat and left the engine running, thankful for the special environmental controls that kept things safe for his furry partner. Late January in Florida tended to be mild, but could sometimes still hit dangerous temperatures. "Sorry, buddy, but I think this is a human-only kind of thing."

Rex grumbled but settled down, his big head resting on his paws when Alex locked the car.

"Are you following me?" The voice came from behind him and sounded hauntingly familiar.

The prickly veterinarian from the bakery.

She was standing where the parking area opened onto the shaded path to the inn's entrance. Her strawberry-blond hair caught the rays of the setting sun, strands blowing in her face with the breeze. Eyes snapping, she waited for him to respond.

"I'm not stalking you, if that's what you mean." His jaw clenched at the insinuation. "I'm a law enforcement officer, not a criminal."

Her face softened slightly, and he caught a glimpse of sadness in her eyes. "Sorry, it's just that in this town, there isn't always a difference."

Chapter Two

Well, that was embarrassing. Cassie truly did try to think before speaking, but some days she was more successful than others. What had she been thinking, accusing him of following her? It had been months since the accident; she needed to stop jumping at shadows.

"Mommy, look what Miss Jillian helped me make!" Cassie's daughter, Emma, came bounding down the stairs of the picturesque inn with the energy and volume befitting a marching band, not a four-year-old. "I made Valentine's cards!"

Behind, at a more sedate pace, came Cassie's best friend and employee, Jillian Caruso. With her mass of black curls and pale skin, she looked like a princess out of a fairy tale, despite her casual jeans and sweater. Right now she also looked a tad guilty. "Before you say anything, this wasn't my fault. I told her I would help her make some, but all the ideas were hers."

Cassie arched an eyebrow, but let it go. She was just grateful Jillian had been willing to entertain Emma. Normally her mom watched Emma after her preschool let out, but today there had been a schedule conflict. Emma was much happier playing at the inn than being stuck with Cassie at the clinic yet again. "Hi, sunshine. I missed you." She swept her up in a hug, letting go of the tension that had dogged her all day. This was why she worked so hard. This little girl was the most important thing in her world and worth all the long hours and missed sleep of the past few months. "Are you having fun?"

"She should be," Jillian broke in. "She's been here less than an hour and we've already played on the playground, looked for seashells on the beach and made brownies."

"Are you a policeman? Did my mommy do something bad?"

Cassie had almost forgotten the deputy behind her. Blushing, she set Emma back down and turned to find him a few feet away, smiling as if she hadn't just bitten his head off.

"Hello, sweetie. I'm Alex. What's your name?"

"I'm Emma. Are you going to take someone to jail?"

"Not today. Unless there are any bad guys here?" His dimples showed when he smiled. Cops should not have dimples.

"Nope, just me and Miss Jillian and Mr. Nic. And Murphy. He's their dog. And a bunch of people for the meeting. But they're going to help kids, so they can't be bad, right?" Her little brows furrowed as she thought.

"Probably not. Helping kids is a good thing. Are you going to help?"

Emma's curls bounced as she nodded. "Yup, I get to help with the decorations. Mommy said so. And I get to come to the big Valentine's Day dance. I'm going to wear a red dress."

"A red dress? Sounds like a great party." He raised his gaze to the third member of the group.

"Hi, I'm Jillian. Welcome to the Sandpiper Inn." She offered her hand to the handsome deputy.

"Nice to meet you. Alex Santiago. Thanks for offering to host the meeting here."

Jillian smiled, her face lighting up. "We're happy to do it. I grew up in foster care myself—I know how hard it can be. Even the best foster families often can't always give the kids as much attention as they need. It will be great if we can get a real mentor program started."

If Alex was surprised by Jillian's casual mention of her childhood, he didn't show it. He just nodded and held out the box he'd picked up at the bakery. "I brought cookies, if you have somewhere I can put them. I figured at least a few people might not have had a chance to grab dinner yet."

Oh, boy. Shame heated Cassie's cheeks. She'd been stereotyping him with the old cops-and-doughnuts line when he'd actually been buying refreshments to share with others—at a charity event, no less.

The sight of the uniform might set her teeth on edge, but that was no reason to be openly rude to him. The car accident that had injured her father so badly had been caused by a single out-of-control deputy, but she couldn't blame the man in front of her just because they both wore the same badge.

"Ooh, can I have a cookie?" Emma looked up at

Alex, practically batting her eyelashes. "I've been very good."

He laughed, and the lines around his eyes softened. "That's up to your mom, princess."

Emma turned pleading eyes to Cassie, whose heart melted. "Since you've been good, yes, one. But just one. Jillian said you've already had a brownie, and I don't want you bouncing off the walls on a sugar high." She nodded a thank you to Alex for letting her make the decision. "Now, let's see those valentines you were telling me about." She brushed off the niggling bit of envy that she hadn't been the one making valentines with her daughter. Maybe that was why Jillian looked concerned about them?

"Cassie, maybe you should wait and read those later?" Jillian cautioned, nodding toward Alex.

Cassie darted a glance at the cop still standing on the stairs with them. He shrugged, then moved past them. "I'll just go find a place to set these down. See you inside."

Why was Jillian acting so tense over this? They were just paper hearts and glitter, not a manifesto. Taking them from Emma's slightly grubby fist, she continued up to the massive front door of the Sandpiper.

The first card boasted a crudely drawn bouquet of flowers, and the words MOM and LOVE circled by pink and purple hearts. "Thank you, sweetie, I love it." She shuffled that one to the back and opened the next one. This time there were happy faces covering the pink paper, and Jillian's name, misspelled, at the center. "Beautiful!" Smiling, she opened the last heart-shaped card and then froze, almost stumbling as her daughter pushed past her into the warmth of the lobby.

The words on the page had instantly imprinted on her brain, but she read them again anyway.

To Daddy. Painstakingly spelled out in red and gold sequins.

She felt a hand on her shoulder. Jillian's eyes were wide with sympathy. "I'm sorry. I didn't know what to do. I told her I'd help her make valentines, but I had no idea…"

Cassie straightened her spine. She'd talk to Emma about it. Make her understand, somehow, that this particular valentine was going to remain unsent. Her head began to throb.

"Don't worry. It's not your fault," Cassie told Jillian. *It's mine.*

Alex kept an eye on the door as he mingled and shook hands in the spacious lobby. Observation was second nature at this point, and he wanted to see how that little scene out front played out. What was the big deal about a couple of valentines? Maybe it was nothing, but an overactive sense of curiosity came with the job.

He was munching on a tiny crustless sandwich when Cassie entered the room. Her daughter and friend followed, but she was the one that drew him, made him want to know more. There was something about the fiery redhead that made her impossible to ignore. Yes, she was pretty in a girl-next-door way, with a petite build and freckled complexion. But it was more than that. Her quick temper should have been off-putting. Instead, her transparency put him at ease. Every emotion showed on her face—there was no hidden agenda. In his line of work, he spent most of his time trying to figure out what someone wasn't saying, but this woman was an open book.

And right now, she looked like she needed a friend. Her pale skin was flushed, and she had a tight look around her eyes, as if she was fighting off a headache. Moving toward her, drawn by instinct more than conscious thought, he offered her a drink. "Water?"

"Hmm?" She looked down at the unopened bottle he held in his hand. "Yes, thank you." Taking a tentative sip, she screwed the cap back on. "Listen, about the coffee shop. I'm sorry I was rude. It was a dumb joke. I just…well, it wasn't about you, specifically."

"Not a fan of cops, are you?"

She winced. "That obvious?"

"Let's see. You made a cop joke in front of a cop. Then you equated law enforcement with criminal behavior. It wasn't a hard case to crack."

Her eyes widened, and then she smiled. A heart-stopping smile that reached her eyes and made him wish he could do more for her than hand her a bottle of water. This must have been how Helen caused all that trouble in Troy. His heart thudded in his chest, warning him to look away.

His eyes landed on her daughter, who had snuck to the far side of the table to liberate another cookie. "She's beautiful."

The smile got even brighter. "Thanks."

"Just like her mother."

Instantly her smile vanished, and her gaze grew guarded. "I should go find a seat, before they're all taken."

He hadn't meant the compliment as a pick-up line, but she obviously thought he was hitting on her and was putting as much space between them as possible. She wasn't wearing a ring, but he'd heard medical people didn't always wear them because of the constant hand-washing. Great. She was probably married. Now she had a reason to dislike him personally, rather than just cops in general.

Unable to come up with a reason to follow her, he hung back to watch the proceedings from the rear of the room, a small crowd filling the seats in front of him. These were his neighbors now, his community. Getting to know them had to be top priority if he wanted to be effective at his job. Hopefully volunteering like this would be a step in that direction. He had other, more personal reasons for wanting to volunteer, but no one needed to know that. He didn't need his past coloring his chances at a future here.

At the front of the room, the woman he'd spoken to earlier, Jillian, stood and called for everyone's attention. "Welcome to the Sandpiper, and thank you for taking the time to help with such a worthwhile project. As most of you know, I was a foster child myself, so I know firsthand how hard that life can be. And what a difference a caring person can make. I'm really thankful we have so many people interested in volunteering, and that, in addition to working with children's services, we will also be partnering with the Palmetto County Sheriff's Department. They will be sponsoring a group of kids for the program as well, kids who are in a difficult spot and might need some extra help. Deputy Santiago is here representing the department tonight and will be volunteering his own time to this important project." She smiled at him, and he raised a hand in acknowledgment. Several of the townspeople turned and sized him up. Many offered warm smiles; a few nodded in acceptance.

Jillian finished, then introduced the chairwoman of the event, Mrs. Rosenberg, a diminutive senior citizen decked out in a leopard-print track suit. As she listed off the various jobs, he made a mental note to sign up for the setup crew. A strong back would be welcome when it came time to move tables and hang decorations, and it sounded a heck of a lot better than messing with tissue paper and glitter for the decorating committee.

Finally, the talking was over. Everyone milled around, catching up on gossip as they waited to sign up on the clipboards on the front table. He started that way, easing through the crowd as best as he could, given that everyone there seemed to want to greet him personally. He'd exchanged small talk with half a dozen people and was less than halfway across the room when he felt a tug on his sleeve.

"Deputy?"

It was the chairwoman, now sporting rhinestone spectacles and wielding a clipboard.

"Yes, ma'am?"

"You're new in town, aren't you?" The question was just shy of an accusation, and the shrewd eyes behind the glasses were every bit as sharp as a seasoned detective's.

"I am." He extended a hand. "Alex Santiago. Nice to meet you."

She gripped him with a wiry strength, then spoke over his shoulder. "Hold on, Tom, I'll be right there." Turning her attention back to him, she smiled. "I have to go handle that. But don't worry. I'll get you signed up myself."

Grateful that he wouldn't have to fight the crowd, he backtracked to the front door. He was almost there when it hit him. "Mrs. Rosenberg?"

From across the room she turned. "Yes?"

"Which committee are you signing me up for?"

"Oh, all of them, of course."

Of course.

Cassie spent most of the drive home trying to figure out what to say to Emma about her valentines. She still wasn't sure how to explain things in a way a four-year-old could understand, but she'd come up with something. She always did.

She set her purse down on the counter and put the old-fashioned kettle on the stove. "Emma, go put your backpack in your room, and get ready for your bath, please. I'll be right there." It was so late she was tempted to skip the bath part of bedtime, but changing the schedule would undoubtedly backfire and keep the tyke up later in the long run. Besides, after an afternoon romping on the beach and exploring the Sandpiper's sprawling grounds, her daughter was in dire need of a scrub-down.

Enjoying the brief quiet, she kicked off her sensible shoes and opened the sliding door to the patio. The screened room was her favorite part of the house, especially at this time of year. The air was chilly by Florida standards, but still comfortable. Right now she would have loved to curl up on the old chaise with her tea and a cozy mystery, but tonight, like most nights, there just wasn't time.

"Mommy, I'm ready for my bath."

"Okay, I'm coming." Duty called. Taking a last breath of the crisp night air, she caught the scent of the Lady of the Night orchid she'd been babying. It would bloom for only a few nights; hopefully she'd get a chance to enjoy it. But for now, she closed the door and went to find her daughter, stopping to fill her mug with boiling water and an herbal tea bag.

Emma was waiting in the bathroom, stripped down to her birthday suit and clutching her favorite rubber ducky. "Bubbles?" she asked hopefully.

"Bubbles. But only a quick bath tonight. It's late."

The little girl nodded solemnly. "Okay, Mommy."

Cassie's heart squeezed. No matter how stressed or tired she was, she never got tired of hearing the word *Mommy* from her baby's lips. She couldn't say she'd done everything right, but this little girl—she had to be a reward for something. She was too good to be anything but that. There was nothing Cassie wouldn't do for her. Which was why it broke her heart to know she couldn't give Emma her biggest wish.

"So did you have fun today at the Sandpiper?" She watched the water level rise around her daughter, the bubbles forming softly scented mountains.

"Yup. I played with Murphy and ate brownies, and we saw a butterfly, and Mr. Nic pushed me super high on the swings."

Nic was Jillian's husband. He had bought the Sandpiper for Jillian just a few months ago, and the playground was one of the first things he'd added to the grounds. He and Jillian were hoping for a child of their own soon, but in the meantime the paying guests—and Emma—made good use of it. "That sounds like a real adventure."

"Uh-huh. And then Miss Jillian helped me make

my valentines. I made one for her, and you, and for a daddy. We just need to get one so I can give it to him."

Darn. The child hadn't forgotten, not that Cassie was surprised. Emma had perfect recall when it came to what she wanted. Now to figure out a way to let her down without breaking her heart. "Honey, I can't just go get you a daddy."

Emma frowned up at her.

Okay, that didn't work. "You are going to have a wonderful Valentine's Day. You're going to have a party at school with cupcakes and candy and everything. And then we'll go to the big dance. It's going to be great, you'll see."

"It would be better if I had a daddy. Then he could be our valentine. Like Mr. Nic is Jillian's valentine. I heard him say so."

Cassie blinked back the sudden sting of tears. She'd tried to be everything for Emma, to provide enough love for two parents, but the older Emma got, the more she realized something was different. Something, someone, was missing.

"A daddy would be nice," she conceded. "But you have me. And we're a great team, you and I. So if you don't have a daddy right now, that's okay, because we have each other, right?"

Emma looked thoughtful, her nose crinkling as she considered. "But why don't I get to have a daddy? Lots of kids at school have one."

The pounding behind Cassie's eyes returned with a vengeance. Rubbing her temples, she tried to explain to her daughter what she still didn't understand herself. "That's just how it is sometimes. Some kids have mommies, and some kids have daddies, and some kids have both."

"Oh, and some kids don't have a mommy or a daddy, right? That's why we get to have the Share the Love party, to help them, right, Mom?"

Cassie sighed in relief. "Right, honey. Those kids are in foster care with people that take care of them until they get a new mommy and daddy. Every family is different, and we just have to be happy about the one we have."

Her face falling, Emma nodded slowly. "Okay."

Watching her daughter's solemn expression, Cassie felt like she'd kicked a puppy. The guilt sat heavy in the pit of her stomach, reminding her of how her choices had led to this. Her impulsiveness, her recklessness, had created this situation. For the millionth time, she fought the instinct to regret ever meeting her lying ex. But of course, without him, there would be no Emma. And that was simply unthinkable. Being a single parent was hard, but it was worth it.

That didn't mean that she didn't sometimes wish she had a partner in all of this. As she toweled Emma off and got her ready for bed, she wondered what it would have been like to have a man to talk to once her daughter was asleep. Instead of eating ice cream out of the carton, she'd have someone she could talk things out with, someone to share her fears and frustrations with.

But letting someone into her life, relying on him like that, was too big a risk. She'd let her emotions carry her away once, and look how well that turned out. No, she needed to keep doing what she was doing and leave the idea of romance alone. She wasn't any good at it, and she couldn't afford to make that kind of mistake again.

Chapter Three

Alex was still shaking his head over Mrs. Rosenberg's sign-up shenanigans ten hours later. And puzzling over the intriguing veterinarian, despite the way she'd blown him off. She was fire and ice, and definitely not interested, but he couldn't quite get her out of his head. Between her and Mrs. Rosenberg, the island definitely had its share of headstrong women.

He'd spent the long night patrolling the quiet streets of Paradise and the connecting highway across the bridge, alone except for Rex and his own thoughts. He was grateful for the lack of crime, but the slow shift gave him too much time to think, too much time to remember the chain of events that had brought him here. Not that this was a bad place to be.

When he'd accepted the position with the Palmetto County Sheriff's Department, he'd expected to be working at the county headquarters in Coconut Bay. Instead he'd been assigned to the small substation serving Paradise. The island was too small to support a city police force, so it, like some of the rural ranching areas across the bridge on the mainland, was under county law enforcement.

As dawn approached, he made a last loop along the beach road to catch the sunrise over the ocean. Stopping in one of the many parking spaces that bordered the dunes, he got out and stretched, his neck popping loudly. At Rex's insistence, he opened the back door as well, snapping the dog's leash on and walking him to a grassy area to relieve himself. When the dog had emptied his bladder, they strolled together to one of the staircases that led down to the sand.

Here he had an unobstructed view of the water and the already pink sky that seemed to melt along the horizon, the water turning a molten orange as the fiery sun crept up to start the day. Sipping from the lukewarm coffee he'd picked up a few hours ago at a gas station on the mainland, he let himself enjoy the quiet. No jarring static from the two-way radio, no traffic, just the soft sound of the waves rolling on the sand and Rex's soft snuffling as he investigated the brush along the stairway.

Alex had made a habit of doing this since he moved here. In the clear morning light, he could feel good about himself, his job, the direction his life was taking. The fresh start to the day was a reminder of his own fresh start, one that he hadn't asked for, but probably needed.

He was over thirty now, as his mother never failed to remind him. Maybe here he'd find a life beyond his work. He wasn't a family man; nothing in his background had prepared him for that kind of life, but a place like Paradise made him want to settle down a bit, make some friends, maybe join a softball team or something.

Chuckling at the image, he turned to go. Rex, trained to stay with him, uncharacteristically resisted the tug on the leash. Maybe he was tired, too.

"Here, boy! Come on, it's quitting time. Let's go."

The dog stood his ground, whiskers trembling as he stared into the dark space under the steps.

"What it is it, boy?" Alex found himself lowering his voice, catching the dog's mood. He was no dog whisperer, but obviously there was something under the stairs. Something more than the broken bottles and fast-food wrappers that sometimes got lodged there.

"Is somebody there?"

There was a scrambling sound, but no answer.

Rex whined, the hairs on his back standing up in a ridge. Feeling a bit silly, but not willing to take a chance, Alex removed his Glock from its holster, finding confidence in its weight even as he sent a silent prayer he wouldn't have to use it. Crouching down, he aimed his flashlight under the wooden structure, his gun behind it. He couldn't see anyone, but there was an alcove under a support beam that was hidden from his light. He'd have to go around.

He circled around to the other side, leaving Rex pacing back and forth at the foot of the stairs. Repeating his crouch and waddle move from before, Alex inched up under the overhang, scanning the area with his light. Nothing.

Woof!

Alex jumped, rapping his head on the rough boards

of the stairway. A lightning bolt of pain shot through his skull as he quickly crab-crawled back out of the cramped space beneath the stairs. He heard Rex bark again and rolled the rest of the way out, careful to keep the gun steady.

"What is it, boy?"

A quick series of staccato barks answered him from the landing above.

"Stop! Sheriff's Deputy." The logical part of his mind knew that it was probably just a kid sneaking a smoke or a surfer who had passed out after too many drinks, but he'd had more than one close call in his career and wasn't going to chance it. Standing up, cursing the sand spurs now embedded in his skin, he followed the dog's line of sight.

There, clearly visible in the breaking dawn, was the menace that had his dog, and him, so worked up. A tiny kitten, barely more than a ball of fluff, was huddled against the top step.

"Rex, hush!" he commanded, not wanting the big dog to scare it back under the stairs. He was not going into those sand spurs again if he could help it.

The kitten was gray, its fur nearly the same shade as the weathered boards he was clinging to. If Rex hadn't made such a fuss, the kitten could have been directly underfoot and Alex would have missed it. Putting the dog into a down-stay, he dropped the leash and tucked away the gun and flashlight. Then he eased up the stairs as quietly as his heavy boots would allow.

The kitten watched him, eyes wide, but didn't run. A small mew was its only reaction, and even that seemed half-hearted. The pathetic creature looked awfully weak. The temperature was only in the mid-forties right now and had been significantly colder overnight. Plenty of strays did just fine, but this one seemed way too small to be out in the cold on its own.

Scooping the kitten up, he cradled it against his chest with one hand, then leaned down and retrieved Rex's leash with the other. The kitten was trembling, obviously cold if nothing else. Loading Rex into the car, he mentally said goodbye to the sleep he'd intended to catch up on. It looked like he was going to be seeing that pretty veterinarian again after all.

Cassie stared at the teakettle with bleary eyes, as if she could make the water boil faster through sheer force of will. She'd tossed and turned again last night. Maybe at some point she'd get used to the nightmares.

She often dreamed about the accident that had left her father in the hospital and herself with a mild concussion and a mountain of worry. At first, they'd feared her father's injuries were permanent, but he was home now and steadily getting better. She'd hoped that would be enough to stop the dreams from haunting her. But so far, no such luck.

But last night the dream had changed. The broken glass and screeching tires were the same as always, brought back in minute detail to terrorize her, but this time the sirens had triggered something new. Instead of the middle-aged deputy who was normally part of the nightmare, there was someone else. Alex Santiago, the new deputy she'd embarrassed herself in front of.

Suddenly, instead of ambulances and flashing lights, there had been stars and the crash of the ocean. They were alone on the beach, kissing as if there was nothing more important than the feel of skin against skin, tongue against tongue. She'd been unbuttoning his uniform when the blaring of her alarm had woken her up.

She had lain there, hot and trembling, for several minutes before forcing herself to shut the dream out of her head. There was probably some deep, psychiatric reason her subconscious was twisting her nightmare into something totally different, but there'd been no point in lying there, trying to figure it out.

So she'd forced herself out of bed and into a quick shower before throwing on her usual uniform of casual khaki pants and a simple cotton blouse. Now she was desperate for some tea and maybe a bite of breakfast. She had another thirty minutes before Emma would be waking up, and she intended to enjoy the quiet while she could.

The tea was still steeping in her mug when she heard a knock at the door. Dunking the bag one last time, she tossed it in the trash as she made her way to the front of the house. Peering through the wavy glass of the peephole, she could just make out the blue uniform of the Palmetto County Sheriff's Department. Her mouth turned dry, another flashback threatening her still drowsy mind.

Her heart thudded hollowly as she turned the lock. Why would there be a cop on her doorstep? Had something happened to her parents? The clinic? A neighbor? Her mind darted through possible scenarios as she opened the door. Surely this wasn't because of the accident? In the beginning, there had been what seemed like countless interviews and questions, but that had all ended months ago.

Taking a deep, cleansing breath, she swung open the door. There on the stoop was Alex, looking just as he had in her dream. The fear retreated, chased off by other, equally potent stirrings. Her cheeks heated in embarrassment, not that he could possibly know that she'd dreamed about him. Keeping her voice cool, she asked, "Is there a problem, Deputy?"

He smiled at her, all male energy and smooth charm. "I suppose it's too early for this to be a social call?"

"I'd say so." She noticed the shadows under his eyes and realized he'd probably just come off the night shift. "I'm assuming you have a professional reason for banging on my door at dawn. If you could share it so I can get back to my breakfast, that would be helpful."

Before he could answer her, she caught the weirdest impression of movement under his department-issued windbreaker. "What on earth?"

At that moment, a tiny, gray head squirmed out of the neck of the jacket and nuzzled his chin. Darn. Now she had to let him in.

"I know it looks strange, but the little guy was shivering. I thought I could keep him warm in my jacket, but he doesn't want to stay put." He grabbed hold of the kitten as it wriggled its way farther out of the coat.

"Well, come on in. Let's take a look at him." She motioned for him to continue back to the kitchen, then shut the door behind him. "Where did he come from and how long ago did you find him?" She kept her tone and actions professional, using her clinical manner to maintain some emotional distance. He might look like a Latin movie star, but the Palmetto County Sheriff's Department logo on his shirt was a glaring reminder of the chaos she was currently embroiled in. She'd help the kitten, then send him on his way, before he or the animal got too close.

Alex followed her, his large stature making her cozy cottage feel small. "Rex found him under one of the beach access staircases. We'd stopped for a few minutes and he refused to leave. Somehow he knew the little guy needed help."

"Is Rex your partner?" The name didn't ring a bell.

"Yeah," Alex answered distractedly as he attempted to remove the kitten's claws from his uniform shirt. "He's waiting out in the car."

"He didn't want to come in?" Had the animosity toward her gotten that bad?

"Oh, he wanted to, but I figured it was better not to totally overwhelm you at this hour of the morning."

Right. More likely his partner just wanted to avoid her. Well, too bad. She was tired of feeling like a pariah in her own town. "It's going to take me a little while to check the kitten out, so you might as well tell Rex to come in. No reason to sit out in the cold."

"You're sure?"

"Of course."

While he fetched his partner, she went to the hall closet to retrieve her medical bag. It was on the top shelf, wedged next to a box of random sports equipment. And a bit too heavy to snag one-handed. She was on her toes, the kitten snuggled firmly in one arm, when she heard the front door open behind her.

Giving up, she turned around to ask for help. "Hey, could one of you hold the kitten while I—"

Her voice died in her throat. Standing directly in her path was the largest German Shepherd she had ever seen, taking up most of the limited real estate in her tiny foyer. Suppressing a completely unprofessional squeal at the sudden intrusion, she cautiously observed the behemoth before deciding the doe-eyed canine meant no harm. Probably. Intuition and years of experience gave her the courage to edge around him, keeping the kitten out of his reach, just in case.

She was relieved to find Alex in the foyer, apparently not eaten by the mammoth canine. "You aren't going to tell me Rex found that guy under a staircase, too, are you?" No way was this regal giant a foundling.

"What?" Alex's eyes narrowed in confusion. "Found who?"

She waved her arm toward the dog. "Him. Where did he come from? Obviously your partner didn't find him when he found the kitten."

Alex's full-throated laugh filled the air, erasing the tired lines that had creased his face a moment before. Unable to resist smiling along with him, she rubbed the kitten's head with her free hand and waited to be let in on the joke.

"Rex is my partner." When she only raised her eyebrows, he continued, "I mean, the dog is Rex. My partner."

Understanding belatedly wound its way through her sleepy brain. "You're a K-9 officer?"

"Yeah. I just assumed a local veterinarian would have known that."

She thought back. She *had* heard rumblings of a new K-9 unit, but she would have sworn the idea had been tabled when it was determined there wasn't enough money in the budget. "I thought the department couldn't afford a K-9 unit? Trained dogs have to cost a fortune."

Alex ruffled the big dog's fur, a wry smile on his face. "He's worth every penny, but you're right. He's way outside Palmetto County's price range. The department was able to get federal and state grants to cover the purchase cost, and Miami-Dade County let me train with its K-9 unit on my off time before I came. The department still has to foot the ongoing costs for veterinary care and our continued training, but that's less expensive than paying the salary for another officer. In the long run, having a K-9 on staff should save the department manpower and money."

Watching Alex's eyes shine with pride in his job and his dog had her swallowing hard. She'd been too quick to think she was being avoided, to assume she was being treated badly. Had she gotten so cynical that she assumed the worst of everyone?

If so, she needed to stop. That wasn't who she wanted to be or what she wanted to teach her daughter. Which meant she needed to bite the bullet and at least try to be open-minded, try to be friendly. Even with the sexy cop standing in her living room.

If Alex had been a little less tired, maybe he would have picked up on Cassie's confusion earlier. As it was, the look on her face when she'd found the hundred-plus-pound dog in her house had been priceless. He gave her credit, though; she'd stood her ground without flinching. She'd correctly read Rex's body language and known he wasn't a threat, despite his size. Heck, even some of his fellow officers were skittish around Rex.

Tough and beautiful. A dangerous combination. He'd once described his ex, a fellow cop, the same way. Then she'd dropped him for an assistant DA and he'd shifted his assessment from tough to cold-hearted. But Cassie, although she'd been less than friendly when he'd first met her, didn't seem to have the calculating nature that had doomed his relationship with his ex. Cassie tried to hide them, but her emotions were right there on the surface, reflected on her face like the rays of the sun off the ocean.

She had her eyes closed as she felt her way over the kitten's body from head to tail. Watching her slender but capable fingers skim the soft fur had him wondering what her touch would feel like. Her husband, if she did turn out to be married, was one lucky bastard.

Who probably wouldn't be happy to find a stranger staring at his wife this way.

Not that she'd even noticed. She'd all but forgotten Alex. Her brows knit in concentration. All her focus was on her small, purring patient.

Better take it down a notch. Focus on the issue at hand. "Is he going to be okay?"

Cassie made a noncommittal noise, then slid the earpieces of a stethoscope into place. A few tense minutes later, her face relaxed into an easy smile. "Lungs sound good, no evidence of any kind of infection, and his heart sounds great. At least, what I can hear over the purring." She nuzzled her face against the now ecstatic creature. "He seems none the worse for wear, just hungry and cold. It's lucky you found him when you did—the forecast is calling for another cold front to roll in by the end of the day."

He suppressed a shudder, despite the warmth of Cassie's cozy kitchen. An image of the kitten, all alone in the cold, flashed through his head, and he made a mental note to pick up one of Rex's favorite chew bones at the store later. The big dog deserved a reward, for sure.

As if reading his mind, Cassie opened a whitewashed cupboard and pulled out a box of dog biscuits.

"Can the hero here have a treat?"

"Of course. He's off duty, and he's definitely earned it."

"What about you?" She tipped her chin toward the kettle on the stove. "I've got hot water for tea, or I can make a pot of coffee. If you have time, I mean."

"Tea would be fine, thank you." He normally stuck to coffee, but there was no point in her making a whole pot just for him. Maybe the coffeepot was strictly for her husband, although it didn't look as if it had been used yet this morning. Her mug, purple with pink paw prints on it, sat alone on the empty counter, smelling of peppermint and flowers.

Come to think of it, there'd only been one car in the driveway. Her husband could have left for work already, but there was nothing in the kitchen to indicate a male presence. Surreptitiously, he scanned the room. No dirty breakfast dishes, no mugs other than hers. Even more telling, the decor ran to pastels and flowers. The evidence was circumstantial, but certainly enough to introduce reasonable doubt as to the existence of a Mr. Marshall.

Accepting the tea, he told himself it didn't matter one way or the other. She'd made her opinion of him, and his profession, perfectly clear when they first met. But as he sat across from her in the cozy kitchen, his dog at their feet and a kitten in her lap, a new, friendlier relationship seemed possible. Which didn't explain why he cared if she shared her home, or her bed, with another man.

He'd obviously been up too long. That was all. Sleep deprivation could mess with your mind. Everyone knew that. After a few hours' sleep, he'd remember all the reasons he wasn't looking for a relationship, especially with the firecracker of a redhead sitting across from him. For now, he'd drink his tea and enjoy a few minutes of company before going home to his empty apartment.

When he'd first taken the job in Paradise, he'd suggested he and his mother share a place, but she'd just chuckled and said he would need his own space for "entertaining." Right. He'd had only one other person in his apartment since he moved to Paradise, and that was the cable guy. Between the new job and the extra training sessions he'd signed up for with Rex, he hadn't had the time or energy for dating. Which was fine by him.

Although right now, enjoying the morning light with a beautiful woman, he wondered if he wasn't missing out after all.

Unwilling to explore that thought, he finished his tea and stood, the chair scraping against the terrazzo floor.

Startled by the noise, the kitten leaped onto the table, nearly overturning the china cups.

"Sorry about that. I'll get this guy out of your hair and be on my way." He scooped up the kitten with one hand. "Thanks for checking him out—I didn't know where else to take him."

Cassie stood to escort him out. "What will you do with him now?"

Good question. One he hadn't thought through yet. He'd been worried about the little guy making it. "I'll have to keep him for a few days, I guess, while I ask around, try to find him a home." Frustrated, he rubbed his eyes with his free hand. "Guess I'd better stop and pick up some food for him first." He nearly groaned with frustration. His tired body was crying out for a bed, but he couldn't let the little guy starve.

"The stores won't even be open for another hour." Cassie's eyes went from man to kitten. "I can take him to the office with me, get him fed, wormed and cleaned up, and then you can pick him up before you start your shift tonight. How does that sound?"

"Like you're my guardian angel. Thank you."

She blushed, the pink accentuating her soft coloring. "I'm not doing it for you. I'm doing it for him." Her firm tone was a contrast to the camaraderie they'd shared in the kitchen. The friendly interlude was over, it seemed.

"Either way, I appreciate it just the same. What time do you need me to come get him?"

"The clinic closes at six, so any time before then is fine."

He could get a solid stretch of sleep and still have time to get food and the cat before his shift started. Thank heaven for small favors. And the angels who delivered them.

Cassie had spent way too much time thinking about Alex today. Really, any time thinking about Paradise Isle's newest lawman was too much. But between Emma's incessant questions over breakfast and the knowing looks and suggestive remarks from her staff, she'd found her attention forced to him more times than she could count. Not that it took much forcing. The sight of the rough-around-the-edges deputy cuddling an orphaned kitten had triggered something inside her, reminding her she was still a woman, not just a mother and veterinarian.

She eyed the gray bundle of fur that had triggered today's chain of events. "You're a troublemaker, you know that?"

The kitten in question was currently exploring her office after being evicted from the patient care area by Jillian. "He hates the cage and his crying is getting the other patients upset," she had said when she'd deposited him on her desk an hour ago.

Absently, Cassie balled up a piece of paper and tossed it in front of the cat. Thrilled, the tiny predator pounced on it, rolling head over heels in his enthusiasm.

Once upon a time, she'd been that carefree, that eager to chase adventure. But she'd been knocked down too hard to be willing to risk tumbling end over end again. She almost envied the kitten its bravery. He'd nearly frozen to death last night and yet he still seemed fearless. Meanwhile, she was afraid of her own shadow most days.

Having her ex leave her had made it hard to trust people, but the aftermath of the car accident she and her father had been in certainly hadn't helped. Naively, she'd assumed that the drunken deputy who hit her would face jail time, that he would pay for his actions. Instead, he'd gotten what seemed like a slap on the wrist. She'd tried to push for more, pointing out Jack's obvious alcoholism, but the department had closed ranks around him. According to them, he'd made a simple mistake and she was just stirring up trouble. A few people had even suggested the accident might have been her fault, despite all evidence to the contrary. Logically, she knew they were wrong, but that didn't make the nightmares or the guilt any better.

"Hey, Cassie?" Mollie, her friend and the clinic receptionist, spoke over the intercom. "Emma's here."

Cassie glanced at her watch. How was it already five o' clock? "Send her back and let her know her little friend is still here." Her daughter had fallen in love with the kitten when she saw it this morning. She'd be thrilled it hadn't been picked up yet.

"Mommy!" Her daughter flew into the tiny office, tossing her backpack down to give Cassie a big hug. "Mollie said he's still here! Where is he?"

Cassie laughed and pointed to the wastebasket in the corner of the room. "Look behind the trash can. I think he'd hiding back there."

Emma, always excited by a new visitor to the clinic, scrambled out of Cassie's lap to check it out. "Found him!" she whooped, clutching the kitty to her chest.

"Careful. Don't squeeze him too hard."

"I know that, Mom. I'm not a baby." The indignation on her little face was better suited to a teenager than a preschooler, but she did have a point. Emma had grown up with foster animals and convalescing pets around the house and knew how to handle them.

"Well, this one is a bit of a troublemaker, so just be careful." Even as she gave the warning, the little guy was trying to climb out of Emma's arms and to scale the mini-blinds over the window. Delighted at his antics, Emma gently untangled him.

"You sure do get into trouble," she scolded the kitten. "That should be your name—Trouble."

Cassie laughed. "I think you're right. That's the perfect name. I'll have Mollie put that on his chart."

"Will the policeman mind that we named the kitten without him?"

"I'm sure he won't mind." Time for a change in subject. "So did you have a good day at school?" Emma had started half days at the preschool affiliated with their church only a few months ago.

"Oh, yeah! John Baker brought a snake into school today for show-and-tell."

"A real snake?" She shivered. There was a reason she hadn't specialized in exotic medicine, and that reason was snakes. Professionally she knew they were legitimate pets, but personally she found them cringe-worthy.

Her daughter nodded with glee. "Uh-huh, a baby one. He had stripes and was really pretty. Can we have a snake, too? I'd take really good care of it."

"Absolutely not. No snakes."

"But you said we could get a pet ages ago and we still don't have one." She stuck her lip out in a perfect pout.

"We will when the time is right."

"When will that be?"

When? When her father was able to work again? When the nightmares went away?

"Soon."

Emma shot her a disbelieving look and went back to snuggling the kitten.

Great, just one more way she'd let her daughter down.

Alex had overslept, then cut himself in his hurry to shave and shower. Now he was standing in the pet food section of Paradise's only grocery store, still bleeding, and confused as heck. Was growth food the same as kitten food? Or should he get the special indoor formula? Or sensitive? What did that even mean, sensitive? And then there were all the hairball options. By the looks of it, half of America's cats were fighting some kind of hair trauma he had no desire to understand.

Dabbing again at the cut on his jaw, he decided on

the bag marked Growth, mainly because it had a picture of a kitten on the front. That had to be a good sign.

Taking the smallest bag, he added it to his basket, which already contained a box of protein bars, new razor blades and the chew bone he'd promised Rex this morning. Thankfully, the checkout line was short, and he was in the car and tearing into one of the protein bars in a matter of minutes. He washed down the makeshift meal with some bottled water and nosed the vehicle south on Lighthouse Avenue. A few quick blocks later and he was pulling into the small parking lot.

Rex woofed hopefully.

"All right, you can come in." He got out and then let Rex out, snapping on his leash. The dog trotted at his side, nose working the breeze. The K-9 was probably picking up a full buffet of smells from all of the pets that had been through there recently.

Once inside, Rex honed in on the treat container in the reception area, sitting prettily directly in front of it.

"Hi, handsome!" The pretty brunette behind the counter, Mollie, according to her name tag, smiled at the panting dog, then turned to Alex. "You must be the man that rescued the kitten this morning, right?"

"Guilty as charged. Although really Rex was the one who found him. He deserves all the credit."

"I'm not sure *credit* is the word." She made a wry face. "Maybe *blame* would be more accurate. That little guy has been driving everyone nuts all day. They had to move him into Cassie's office because he was getting the other patients all worked up with his yowling."

Alex winced. "Sorry. I probably should have taken him with me, but I wasn't exactly prepared for a surprise kitten at six this morning."

"Don't be silly. It's not your fault he's so rambunctious. And Dr. Marshall's daughter is in love with him. She's back there playing with him now."

"Emma's here? Surely her mother doesn't bring her to work every day?"

The receptionist tipped her head, studying him. "I didn't realize you'd met Emma already. Her grandparents dropped her off a little bit ago. They watch her in the afternoons."

He nodded. "Emma and I met at the Share the Love meeting the other day—she asked if I was going to take anyone to jail. She's quite the character."

Mollie laughed. "That she is. Not a shy bone in her body, that's for sure. Have a seat. I'll let them know you're here."

Alex chose the seat farthest from the door, across from an older man snuggling a Persian cat. Rex ignored the cat, preferring to keep an eye on the treat jar.

Only a few minutes later, he was called into an examination room. He was surprised to recognize one of the owners of the Sandpiper, Jillian, waiting for him, dressed in scrubs.

"Deputy Santiago, good to see you again." She offered a wide smile, then crouched down to pet Rex. "And nice to meet you, Rex. I hear you're quite the hero."

"He's going to get a swollen head from all the compliments the women in this place give him. And call me Alex."

"Okay, Alex. Well, Dr. Marshall should be with you in just a minute. She was checking on the kitten's lab results, but he seems plenty healthy."

"Yeah, I heard he's been a handful. Sorry about that."

"Please. If we can't handle a two-pound kitten for a few hours, we're in trouble."

"Well, thank you anyway. I have to admit, I'm surprised to see you here. I thought you ran the Sandpiper?"

"Oh, no, I'm one of the owners, but my husband's the one who really runs it. Nic grew up in the hotel business, so he handles all the day-to-day stuff. I've been working here in the clinic since I was in high school. I can't imagine doing anything else."

He nodded in understanding. He could respect that; it was how he felt about being a cop.

The door opposite the one they came in from opened and Cassie entered, her daughter behind her. In Emma's arms was the kitten.

"He looks better," Alex commented. "Jillian said he's doing okay now."

"He's doing more than okay," Cassie told him. "He's got a belly full of food and has been given more attention today than he's probably ever had in his life."

As if to prove her statement, the kitten began purring, his throaty rumbling surprisingly loud given his small size.

"That's good, because he's going to be on his own tonight. I did stop and get him some food. And I can make him a bed up, with towels or something."

"Good. What kind of litter did you get?"

Uh-oh. "Um, well…"

Cassie watched his face, then burst into laughter. Her shoulders shook as she spoke. "You've never had a cat before, have you, Deputy?"

Her laughter was almost worth the embarrassment. Almost. He had a college degree and had solved numerous criminal cases, yet he couldn't figure out how to take care of a simple cat? She must think he was an idiot.

Still chuckling, she put a hand on his arm. "I'm sorry I laughed. I should have given you a list this morning or at least told you what to get."

Her hand on his arm was warm, the casual touch sending a jolt of heat through his body. Pulling away, he cleared his suddenly dry throat. "You did more than enough. This was my fault." He rubbed a hand over his jaw. "I don't suppose you sell that stuff here? I've got to be on patrol in a bit, and, well—"

"Why don't we take Trouble home with us, Mommy?"

Alex looked from the bright-eyed girl to her mother. "I don't think—"

"Please, Mommy? You said we would get a pet. And this one needs a home. And he loves me so much, I know he'd miss me. And," she said, pointing at Alex triumphantly, "he doesn't know how to take care of a cat. He doesn't even have a litter box."

Put in his place by a child. So much for making a good impression. He'd be offended, except she was right. He had no idea what to do with a cat. He'd grown up with dogs, but cats were a new experience. Still, he didn't want to put Cassie out more than he already had.

"I'm sure I can figure something out for tonight, and I'll pick up a book at the library tomorrow. It can't be that hard, right?"

Cassie nodded slowly, but her eyes were on her daughter. Remembering her earlier conversation with Emma, she gave Alex a half-hearted smile. "I'm sure you could figure it out, but Emma's right. I did promise her a pet." And since she couldn't give her a dad, she might as well give her a cat. Because that made sense. Not.

"Really, Mommy? Really-really?"

"Really-really. But you'll have to take care of him yourself. He'll need to be fed and his litter box scooped. It won't just be about playtime and snuggles." Her lecture was lost on the girl, who was already whispering into the kitten's ear. No doubt they were planning all sorts of adventures.

"You didn't have to do this. I would have managed."

Alex looked uncomfortable with the change in plans. The poor guy probably wasn't used to being overruled by a four-year-old.

"I'm sure you could have handled it, but Emma's right. I did promise her a pet. I've been saying it for a while now, and since we aren't fostering any pets right now, it's a good time to do it. And a kitten's better than a snake."

"A snake?" He arched an eyebrow.

"It's a long story." A thought struck her. "You didn't want to keep him yourself, did you? I really should have asked before basically catnapping him from you."

He grinned at her pun, one side of his mouth tipping up higher than the other. The crooked smile made him look boyish and devious all at once. A potent combination that had her pulse tripping faster. "No, I wasn't planning to keep him. Between the new job and Rex, I'm not looking to take on any more responsibilities."

Her libido cooled as quickly as if he'd dumped a bucket of ice water on her. Avoiding responsibility was a definite turnoff. "Right, well, it's good you know your limitations. Too many people don't take that into account until after the damage is done."

"I just want to do right by the little guy. If you and Emma are willing to give him a good home, well, I can't imagine a better place for him." He paused. "Do you need to run this by your husband before bringing a new pet home? I don't want to cause any problems."

She fumbled with the stethoscope around her neck. "No, that won't be necessary."

"It's just Mommy and me at home," Emma piped up. "We're a team."

Cassie was used to looks of pity when people found out she was a single mom, but Alex's eyes showed only admiration.

Turning back to Emma, he crouched down so he could look her in the eye. "Well, then. Do I have your word that you're going to take good care of him? Feed him and clean up after him and whatever else your mama says?"

Her eyes wide, she nodded solemnly. Then, without warning, she ambushed him with a hug, nearly knocking him, the kitten and herself to the floor. "Thank you for finding Trouble, and for giving him to me! He's the best present ever!"

No one could resist Emma when she turned on the cute, not even a hardened lawman like Alex. He hugged the girl right back. Then, once she released him, he stood and called Rex to his side. "Rex here is the one who found your kitty."

Awed by the massive dog, she asked quietly, "Does he like little girls?"

"Of course he does. Little girls are his favorite kind of people."

That was all the encouragement Emma needed. She wrapped her arms around the giant dog's neck, burying her face in the thick fur. Cassie started forward, visions of police dogs and bite suits flashing through her mind.

Alex stopped her with a touch. "They're fine."

He was right. Rex had his tongue lolling out of his mouth, panting in the way of happy dogs everywhere.

"I'm sorry. I normally wouldn't worry, but I haven't had much experience with police dogs. I wouldn't want—"

"No need to explain, I get it. Honestly, I wouldn't suggest she try that with most K-9s, but Rex really likes kids. I've even done some demonstrations at the school. He was chosen for our department partly because he's so social. He's the first dog here, and if he gets a bad reputation, that would be the end of the Palmetto County K-9 unit."

As she watched the dog, her instincts agreed with Alex's words. Rex did seem as comfortable with Emma as any family pet.

"You take Rex to schools?" Emma had lifted her head to speak, but kept her arms around the dog.

"Sometimes." He winked, then stage-whispered, "I think he likes to show off."

Oh, my. The combination of the wink and the dimples, not to mention the low gravel of his voice, had Cassie clutching the edge of the exam table. This man was so potent he needed a warning label.

"Could you bring him to my school for show-and-tell? That would be even cooler than John Baker's silly snake."

"Well—"

"Emma, Deputy Santiago is a busy man. He and Rex have a very important job to do."

"That's right, we do."

Emma's face fell.

"But show-and-tell sounds pretty important, too. And Rex sure would love to see you again."

Sexy, confident, good with dogs and kids. If she hadn't had a hang-up about the Palmetto Sheriff's department, she would have said he was perfect.

Why couldn't he have been a doctor or a lawyer, or even a mechanic? No, he had to be part of the good old boy network that passed for law enforcement in this area. Yeah, she was cynical. But for good reason, darn it.

Pasting a smile on her face, she remembered this wasn't about her. It was about her daughter. "Thank you, Deputy Santiago. I know the kids will love having you come. I'll have her teacher contact you about the details, if that's okay."

"Sure, no problem at all." Patting Emma's strawberry-blond curls, he extended a hand to Cassie. "Thank you again for taking the kitten. Let me know if it doesn't work out, and I'll figure something else out."

His hand was warm on hers, firm but gentle. Letting go abruptly, she stuck her tingling hand in her pocket. "We'll be just fine, Deputy. Thank you."

As Alex passed by the receptionist's desk, Cassie caught Mollie checking out his rear end, and who could blame her? The deputy said he didn't want to cause trouble, but from where she stood, he was exactly that.

Chapter Four

Alex stood in front of the double doors of All Saints School, feeling as if he was eight years old again. He'd gone to an elementary school very similar to this one and had spent more than his fair share of time in the principal's office. But that was a long time ago, and he was no longer a messed-up little kid in trouble for fighting. He was a grown man; there was no reason to be intimidated.

Rex whined, looking between him and the door. Sometimes having a dog so in tune with his emotions wasn't a good thing.

"It's okay, boy. They invited us. You'll show them your tricks, and then we can go home." He'd scheduled this visit for his day off and was looking forward to a nap and then maybe stopping by his mom's place for dinner. Just the thought of her empanadas had his stomach grumbling.

"All right, let's go." He squared his shoulders and opened the door, stepping into the relative warmth of the building. It even smelled like a school, of crayons, newly sharpened pencils and that odd industrial soap all schools seemed to use.

Rex's nails clicked on the industrial linoleum floor as he walked to the door labeled Administration. An older woman with a neat bob of silver hair sat behind a massive oak desk. Spotting him, she stood as he came in. "Deputy Santiago, I'm Eleanor Trask, the assistant principal. I want to thank you for coming. Our pre-schoolers are really looking forward to this."

"I'm happy to do it."

She stepped past him through the door, motioning him to follow. He walked beside her down the wide hall, then down a side passage with doors every few feet. Paper-plate snowmen with children's names on them lined the walls. He smiled, knowing that most of the artists had never seen a single flake of snow.

"You like children, Deputy?"

"Yes, ma'am, I do. Children are honest, and I don't see much of that in my line of work."

She paused and then nodded. "I've never thought of it quite that way, but you're right. They are honest in a way refreshing to most adults. I find that people who don't like children usually have something to hide."

He thought of his own childhood and agreed. "I suppose that's true."

They stopped in front of a door toward the end of the corridor. "This is it. We decided to bring in the other two preschool classes as well, given the exciting nature of this particular show-and-tell. You should have quite the audience."

Swallowing, he let her open the door and introduce him. From the doorway, he could see about thirty small children seated in rows on the brightly-colored carpet. After Ms. Trask reminded the students to be on their best behavior, she left, leaving him wondering what he'd been thinking. He'd faced hardened criminals less intimidating.

"Hi, Rex!" The familiar voice carried over the whispers of her classmates. Rex woofed in return, setting all the kids into fits of giggles. Emma was front and center, her red-blond curls in pigtails and her face alight with joy. Smiling back, he felt a heavy tug on his heartstrings. It seemed both the Marshall women knew how to get to him.

Alex spent the next half-hour telling the students a bit about police dogs before moving on to some demonstrations. Rex did his various obedience moves, then used his nose to find a hidden object in the room. He determined which of two pencils had been held by Alex. Delighted by the dog's tricks, the children all begged to pet Rex. He let them, one by one, monitoring closely. Rex might like kids, but that many children could overwhelm any dog.

Emma's excitement was contagious. By the end of his talk, all the kids were in love with Rex, and half wanted to be K-9 handlers when they grew up. Definitely a success. Before leaving, he handed out shiny sheriff's deputy stickers, hoping they would keep the kids distracted enough for him to make his getaway. He was just slipping out when Emma stopped him.

"Deputy Alex?"

"Yes?"

"Do you have anyone to be your valentine yet?"

Where on earth did that come from? "Um, no, I guess not. Other than Rex here."

She rolled her eyes at him. "A dog can't be your valentine. It has to be a people."

"Oops, sorry. I guess I don't, then."

"Would you like one?"

Was he being propositioned by a four-year-old? "Um, sure, I guess. I hadn't thought about it much yet."

"Perfect. I'll tell her you said yes." Flush with success, she waved goodbye and ran back to her friends.

Had he just agreed to something? And if so, what?

Cassie managed to snag one of the few open parking spots; maybe that meant her luck was changing. The school secretary had called an hour ago to tell her that Emma had forgotten her lunch again. Stuck in surgery, she hadn't been able to leave until twenty minutes ago, only to find the abandoned Hello Kitty lunchbox on the backseat of her car, tucked under a sweater. And after baking in the hot car all morning, the contents were less than edible. It might be January, but in typical Florida fashion the temperature had climbed twenty degrees in the past few days. Then, what should have been a quick trip to the corner store for more food had stalled out when the person ahead of her paid with loose change—counting and recounting three times.

But she was here now, and lunch period didn't start for another ten minutes. Slamming the car door closed, she made for the main entrance, only to have the door open as she reached for it. Off balance, she did a stutter step to keep from falling.

"Whoa, sorry. Are you okay?"

Alex Santiago and his dog were staring at her, concern showing in both their gazes. How could she have forgotten today was the show-and-tell thing? "I'm fine, really. I just have a habit of tripping over my own feet, that's all."

"Are you sure?"

His deep voice set off tingles in all the right places. Stomping down on her libido before she said something stupid, she held the lunch box out in front of her like a shield. "I'm good. Just going to drop off Emma's lunch. She forgot it this morning. How about you—how was show-and-tell?"

He winced. "Loud. Very loud. I'm not quite sure how such small people make so much noise. But other than that, I think it went well. And Rex put on a good show."

"I'm sure he did." Awkwardly, she ducked past him into the building. "I'll see you around, I guess."

"Oh, you will. Mrs. Rosenberg was helpful enough to sign me up for every committee there is for the Share the Love dance. We're bound to run into each other."

"Mrs. Rosenberg is a force to be reckoned with." Shaking her head at the image of the elderly lady pulling a fast one on the tough cop, she suddenly realized something. "Does that mean you'll be at the decorating committee meeting tomorrow night?"

"So it seems. And you?"

"Yes, that's the only committee I signed up for."

"You've got plenty on your plate already with Emma and the clinic, I'm sure."

"You're right, I do." And yet she'd been standing there making small talk when it was almost time for Emma's lunch. "Speaking of which, I'd better get this to Emma."

"Of course. See you tomorrow." He exited via the door she'd just come through, Rex trotting at his side.

Shaking her head to clear her thoughts, she went to the front office to sign in and get a visitor's pass, then headed for her daughter's classroom. She should have just enough time to say hello before getting back for afternoon appointments. Her own lunch would have to be a protein shake between patients, but that wasn't anything new.

Emma was lining up at the front of the room with her friends, but ran for a hug when she saw Cassie walk in. "Thanks, Mom. Sorry I forgot it."

Cassie guided her back into line and walked with her toward the cafeteria. "You know, one of these days I'm going to just let you starve." Rolling her eyes, Emma reached for her hand as they walked.

They both knew that wasn't going to happen, mainly because Cassie was just as forgetful, if not worse. If she didn't have Mollie to keep her on track at work, she'd be in deep trouble. Sticky notes and alarms on her smartphone were a big help, but it would be a few years before Emma could make use of those. "Just try to be more careful. Okay?"

"I will. I was just so excited about seeing Rex and Deputy Alex that I couldn't think about anything else."

Another shared trait—a fondness for handsome men and good-looking dogs.

"Oh, and Mommy, guess what?"

"What?"

"Deputy Alex is going to be your valentine!"

"What?" Several heads had turned at Emma's enthusiastic statement. No doubt there would be talk in the teacher's lounge later.

"I asked, and he said he doesn't have a valentine. And you don't have one, either. So you can be each other's. It's perfect."

Emma's innocence made Cassie's heart squeeze. "Oh, honey, it's not quite that simple. Just because we're both single doesn't mean we're going to be valentines with each other."

Emma frowned. "Why not? Don't you like Deputy Alex?"

"Of course I do." More than she should. "But someday, when you're a grown-up, you'll understand that things like valentines are more complicated than just liking someone."

"I don't ever want to be a grown-up. It makes everything complicated."

No kidding, kid. No kidding.

Cassie gave Emma a quick hug at the cafeteria door, then headed back out to her car and her very grown-up, way-too-complicated life.

Back at the clinic, Cassie had little time to dwell on her lack of a valentine or her daughter's ridiculous matchmaking. A terrier with kennel cough had one exam room shut down until it could be fully disinfected, causing the rest of the appointments to be delayed. She'd soothed the last cranky client of the day only a few minutes ago and was going over the day's receipts when Jillian knocked on the open door.

"Got a minute?"

Cassie stretched her arms over her head, her vertebrae popping at the movement. "Sure, what's up?"

Her friend pushed her dark curls off her face, fidgeting, her eyes looking everywhere but at Cassie.

Gut clenching, Cassie put down the stack of papers she'd been reading. "What is it? What's wrong?" Jillian was her best friend, the closest she'd ever gotten to having a sister.

Jillian's big brown eyes filled with tears, which she quickly wiped away. "Nothing. I mean, nothing's wrong. It's just…well…" She placed a hand on her flat belly and met Cassie's gaze. "I'm pregnant."

"Oh, my goodness, really?" Jumping up, Cassie stared at Jillian's hand, as if she could see through it to the baby growing underneath. "That's amazing! But why are you crying? I thought you and Nic wanted to have kids right away?" A horrible thought hit her. "The baby's okay, right? And you're okay?"

"We're both fine. I saw the doctor on my lunch hour and she says everything is perfect."

"Oh, thank goodness." She sat back down. "And Nic's happy about the baby?"

"He's over the moon. He was drawing out plans for the nursery when I left."

That sounded like Nic. The former hotel magnate had recently discovered a latent talent for carpentry. "So then why are you crying?"

Laughing through her tears, Jillian shook her head. "I don't know! It just keeps happening."

Relief sang through Cassie. Embracing her friend, she found her own eyes filling. "Hormones will make you crazy, but who cares? You're going to be a mommy! You have to let me throw your baby shower, promise?"

"Of course you can. So you aren't upset?"

Cassie pulled away. "Upset? Why on earth would I be upset?"

"Because of all the inconvenience. I'm not going to

be able to take X-rays, and I think I'll have some limits on lifting, and it's just going to make more work for everyone," she finished with a sob.

"Oh, sweetie, don't worry about all that. Mollie can cross-train some and help out in the back, and you can help her up front. We're all in this together, right?"

A fresh round of tears soaked Jillian's smiling face. "Right. Thanks. And I am happy. I just didn't think it would happen so soon, you know?"

"I've seen the sparks between you and Nic. Honestly, I'm surprised it took this long."

Jillian grinned through her tears. "Speaking of which, I've seen the way that new deputy looks at you, the one with the Shepherd. Anything going on there?"

"Hardly." She turned her gaze back to the paper printouts on her desk.

"Well, why on earth not? He's hot, single and likes dogs." She ticked off the traits on her fingers.

"And works for the sheriff's department. No thank you."

"Cassie, the entire sheriff's department is not against you. Besides, Alex wasn't even working there when all that happened."

"It doesn't matter." She forced a smile. "I've got my hands full anyway, with work and Emma and the charity dance. And on top of all that, I've got a baby shower to plan. Who's got time to think about men with all that going on?"

"Right." Jillian didn't look convinced, but good friend that she was, she dropped the subject. "If you don't have anything more for me, I'm going to go. Nic wants us to call and tell his family about the baby tonight."

"Go, then. I'm almost done here anyway. And congratulations again. You're going to make a wonderful mother."

And she would. Despite Jillian's lonely childhood, bouncing from one foster home to another, or maybe because of it, she would be an excellent mother. And her baby would be lucky enough to grow up with a father, as well. He or she would have two stable, loving parents, the kind of family Emma was so hungry for and Cassie would never be able to offer.

Chapter Five

Alex parked his department SUV in the gravel lot of the Sandpiper and tried to psych himself up for the scrutiny and pointed questions he knew were coming. It wasn't that he disliked socializing, but being the new guy in a small town meant everyone thought they had a right to his life story. Thankfully, so far the gossips had been too well-mannered to press him, but his luck couldn't hold forever.

"Come on, boy. Jillian said you can come in as long as you're nice to her dog."

Rex woofed, nearly toppling Alex in his eagerness to get out and explore. The inn billed itself as pet friendly, and no doubt there were a myriad of smells for the big dog to enjoy. Not to mention, letting him amble a bit on the way in meant a few more minutes before he was put under the microscope by the committee ladies.

Rex was intently sniffing a coco-plum hedge when his ears suddenly pricked up. A moment later, the sound of footsteps on gravel signaled someone coming up the path behind them. The dog's frantic tail wagging indicated a friend, so it was no surprise when Cassie came around the bend. "He remembers you."

"He remembers the treats I gave him, don't you boy?"

Woof.

"Sorry, I don't have any on me right now. But don't worry, I bet Emma will sneak you some out of Murphy's stash."

"Is Emma with you?"

"My mom dropped her off here after dinner, so I wouldn't have to make an extra trip to pick her up."

He angled his steps beside hers as they headed for the main building. "It must be a big help, having your family around."

"I couldn't have done it without them. My dad is a vet, too. He owns the clinic, in fact. But he hasn't been able to work since the accident, leaving me with longer hours. It's a bit better now that Emma's in preschool, but that's only part-time. Knowing she's with family or with a friend like Jillian after school keeps me from going totally insane."

Accident? He was about to ask her about it when the front door swung open. A tall, dark-haired man stepped out and embraced Cassie, nearly sweeping her off her feet.

"Can you believe it? Jillian said she told you today."

Cassie laughed and gave him a peck on the cheek. "Yes, she told me, and of course I can believe it. You two are meant to be parents." She turned back. "Nic, this is Alex Santiago. Alex, meet Nic Caruso, proprietor and father-to-be."

Alex's offered hand was enveloped in a very enthusiastic handshake. "Thanks for letting us use your place for the meeting. It's very generous of you."

"That's all Jillian. She's the one in charge."

Cassie grinned. "And don't you forget it."

"I won't. She won't let me. In fact, I'd better go see if she needs anything else before the meeting starts."

Alex watched him duck through a swinging door into a private hallway. "He seems like a nice guy."

"He is. They're really lucky to have each other."

At her wistful smile, an ache started deep in his chest. Her vulnerability triggered all his protective instincts. Someone had done wrong by this woman, and he wouldn't mind a few rounds alone with whoever it had been.

Breaking the silence, Cassie indicated the French doors that were the rear entrance. "We'd better get started before they get it all done without us."

He followed her gaze across the casual yet elegant room. Overstuffed furniture was arranged around a native coquina-stone fireplace. Beyond that, large windows were open to the crisp night air. Over the sound of the sea came the rise and fall of voices; it seemed everyone else was out back.

As soon as they stepped outside, they were greeted by a chorus of welcomes. Mrs. Rosenberg was there, of course, and she nodded approvingly when she saw them. Jillian was seated next to her at a large picnic-style table, and a number of other women filled the deck chairs scattered along the wide whitewashed porch that wrapped around the building. As expected, he was the only male member of the decorating committee. Well, except for Rex and Murphy, Jillian and Nic's dog. The border collie had been sleeping under the table, but at the sight of Rex had bulleted through his mistress's legs to greet his new playmate.

"Murphy, don't make a pest of yourself. Rex is a serious working dog, not your new partner-in-crime," Jillian admonished. She smiled up at Alex. "Sorry, he means well, but he's still stuck in the puppy phase. Possibly permanently."

"No problem. Rex likes other dogs and could do with a buddy." Rex held still as the younger dog sniffed him all over, then returned the favor. Canine introductions over, they both looked up at Alex, as if waiting for permission to play. "Is it okay if I let him off his leash? I don't want him to get tangled with Murphy."

"Of course. Maybe Rex's good manners will rub off on him. Either way, I've got the gate to the yard closed off, so they can't go far."

At the click of the lead unsnapping, both dogs bounded off for the far end of the porch, away from the crowd. Keeping one eye on the dogs, Alex settled onto a white bench next to Cassie and across from Jillian. "I hear congratulations are in order."

The mother-to-be blushed. "Yes, we just found out. We're both a bit overwhelmed."

"Understandably. I'd be quaking in my boots, but fatherhood never has been on my radar. Nic seems to be taking it in stride, though."

"You didn't see his face when I told him. I thought he was going to pass out right in front of me."

Mrs. Rosenberg patted her hand. "They all get a bit jumpy when they find out. I know my Marvin did. But before you know it they're passing out cigars and acting like they're the first person to ever make a baby."

Next to him, Cassie fiddled with the edge of her sweater. Most of the women he knew loved baby talk, especially the experienced mothers. Cassie, however, looked as if she'd sooner face a firing squad than swap maternity tales. Jillian must have seen it, too, because she took one look at her friend's face and changed the subject.

"Cassie, can you and Alex work on the banners? Mrs. Rosenberg and I are going to go inside and put together the centerpieces."

"Sure." Cassie looked to Alex. "Does that sound okay to you?"

Alex nodded. "Sure, as long as there are some instructions somewhere. I'm kind of clueless with arts and crafts."

Mrs. Rosenberg pointed to the stacks of paper and craft supplies on the table as she stood up. "Cassie knows what to do. Just stick with her and you'll be fine."

He looked expectantly at Cassie. "I hope you're a patient teacher. I'm afraid I failed cut and paste in school."

That got a grin from her. "Well, big guy, you're going to get a crash course in it tonight. Not to brag, but as a surgeon, I'm an expert at precision cutting. All you have to do is watch me."

No worries there. Seeing her there, bathed in moonlight, he couldn't have taken his eyes off her if he tried.

Cassie never would have imagined she'd enjoy spending an evening cutting out hundreds of construction-paper hearts. But talking with Alex had made the time fly by. He'd entertained her with stories of growing up

Puerto Rican in Miami, teasing her when she couldn't pronounce the name of his favorite food. She'd shared some of the funnier animal encounters she'd had over the years, and then they'd both cracked up when Murphy ran in with an entire string of pink twinkle lights wrapped around his body.

After they untangled the dog, he had been banished to Jillian and Nic's private quarters, where he'd kept Emma company watching cartoons. Rex, worn out by the younger, more rambunctious dog, had curled up under the table with his head on Cassie's feet.

In fact, the only awkward part of the evening had been when Jillian and Mrs. Rosenberg were comparing stories about their husbands. They hadn't meant any harm, but remembering her own early pregnancy was hardly a pleasant experience. Nic might have been over the moon about the new baby, but Cassie knew too well that not all men got past the initial shock and fear. Certainly her ex never had. He'd called her a liar, then suggested the baby wasn't his after all. Learning that he'd walked out on her had been almost a relief after the awful things he'd said.

His reaction might have been extreme, but it wasn't all that uncommon, in her view. Even Alex had commented on how frightening the idea of fatherhood was.

Thankfully, once the subject was changed, the rest of the evening had been more pleasant than she'd expected. Now it was probably time to get going. She finished stringing one more heart on the banner in front of her and reluctantly stood up. "It's late. I need to get Emma home and into bed."

He looked down at his watch. "Wow, it is late. She must be exhausted."

"Actually, she's probably passed out on Jillian's bed. She can fall asleep anywhere."

"Seriously?" His eyebrow cocked in disbelief. "We haven't exactly been quiet out here."

"I'm telling you, she could fall asleep in Times Square. The clock strikes eight and she's out for the count. She's been like that since she was a baby. Come, I'll show you."

She grabbed his hand, pulling him up to follow her. Awareness snaked up her arm like heat lightning on a summer's night. Dropping his hand, she stumbled back as if she'd literally been shocked.

Alex stared, the heat in his eyes a match for the surge she'd felt in his touch. All she had to do was lean forward and he'd kiss her, and it had been so long since she'd been kissed.

But a kiss wouldn't be enough, not by half. Accepting that and knowing it couldn't be more, she drew a deep breath and turned away. She wasn't running away. She was being sensible. So why did the sound of his footsteps behind her have her increasing her pace?

She stopped just inside Jillian and Nic's private suite, taking a moment to calm herself before waking Emma up.

"Wow, you were right." Alex's husky whisper sent a shiver down her spine.

Emma was passed out in a heap on the floor, her head resting on Murphy's snoring form. "She's always fallen asleep easily, but she's a bear when you wake her up."

"Then let's not wake her." Alex stepped past her and gently scooped Emma into his arms. Cassie meant to stop him, to insist that she could handle things, but the way his jeans molded to his body when he bent over left her temporarily speechless. Oblivious to her ogling, he effortlessly carried the girl past her and toward the front of the inn. Scrambling after him, she rushed to open the door while waving a hasty goodbye to her friends. Jillian's lips quirked up at the sight, but she thankfully didn't comment.

Outside, the cooler air calmed her senses and her libido. There was no need to get all worked up. Alex was just being chivalrous. But all her rationalizations didn't stop her heart from aching at the sight of her daughter cradled in his strong arms. This was the kind of thing Emma had missed out on by not having a father around.

In the parking lot, Alex silently slid Emma into her car seat, then managed the buckles like a pro.

"Thanks."

"Anytime."

Right. One time was more than was smart, if her jumping pulse was any indication. If she wanted to protect her heart, she was going to have to stay far away from Alex Santiago.

Chapter Six

"So, I hear you met the new K-9 officer?"

Leave it to her dad to touch on the one subject she was hoping to avoid. He'd had a knack for that all her life.

"I've run into him a few times. And he found an abandoned kitten that Emma talked me into keeping." Across the kitchen table in her parents' home, her father watched her carefully.

"Emma told me about that. She's taken quite a shine to him."

"Well, kittens are pretty hard to resist."

"I was talking about the man, not the cat."

Well, he was hard to resist, too. But that was more than her father needed to know. Turning her eyes back to the laptop in front of her, she chose her words carefully. "He seems very nice."

Her father looked over his glasses at her. "Very nice?"

"Yes, he seems nice." No way was Dad going to get her to admit to more than that. She'd come over so they could go over the clinic books together, not so he could play matchmaker.

He leaned over her shoulder and tapped at the keyboard, printing out the most recent month's statistics. "Well, that should make things easier."

"Make what easier?"

"I'm getting to that. You see, before the accident, I'd agreed to help the sheriff's office with the new K-9 unit. Nothing major, just routine checkups and some help with the training runs."

She closed the laptop. Obviously that wasn't why her dad had called her over anyway. No, he had something else up his sleeve.

"So anyway, with me still not up to par, that leaves you."

She stared at him. "Leaves what to me, exactly?"

"Like I said, routine medical care. And some training."

"Medical care, sure. But training? You want me to put on a bite suit or something?" What on earth had her father gotten her into?

"No, nothing like that. But they want the dogs to do search work and need some volunteers. I'd planned on doing it, but as it is…" He pointed to his injured leg.

"Fine. I'll do it." Darn him, he was actually smirking. "You know, you don't have to look so pleased about the whole idea."

"Who, me?" He winked at her. "I really do feel bad about backing out, so I'm glad you're going to take my place. But yes, I am also happy about you spending some time with a young man. A very nice young man, I believe you said."

"Who just so happens to work for the sheriff's department. You know, I wouldn't think you'd be so eager to help them after everything that happened."

"Cassie, honey, we've been over this. You can't hold the whole department responsible for what happened. And this Alex fellow wasn't even here back then."

Logically, she knew her father was right. But that didn't keep her from breaking out into a cold sweat at the sight of the blue sheriff's uniform or jumping every time she heard a siren. She'd made some progress, thanks to a therapist recommended by the ER doctor who had treated her. And it was true that Alex didn't trigger the usual panic. But he caused a whole different kind of emotional overload, one she wasn't up for dealing with.

"I said I'll help. Don't push for more, okay?" She was agreeing at all only because she still felt guilty about the accident. No, she hadn't caused it, but she'd been the one driving, and she couldn't help but second-guess herself. Especially when she saw the pain her father was still in.

"How's the physical therapy going?" She gestured to his knee, now supported by a brace.

"Good." He beamed. "I should be back at work in another week or so."

"Is that what Jen said?" Jen Miller was her father's physical therapist and an old schoolmate.

Her father rubbed the knee absently. "It's what I'm saying. You're doing a tremendous job, but you can't run that clinic on your own forever. That's why I asked you to come over. I can at least start doing the paperwork." He ran a hair through his still-thick gray hair. "If I don't do something, I'm going to go crazy."

"He's right, much as I hate to admit it." Her mom walked in, a load of laundry in a basket on her hip. "I know he enjoys spending time with me and helping with sweet Emma, but if he doesn't get back to the clinic soon, he's going to drive both of us crazy."

Her father snaked out a hand and pulled his still-trim wife into his lap. "Lady, I'm already crazy, over you." He planted a loud kiss on her lips, then let her up.

Cassie turned back to her computer, never sure what to make of her parents' affectionate displays. She was glad they were so happy together; plenty of her friends growing up had come from divorced or unhappy homes. But she couldn't help wonder what was wrong with her, that she had never found that kind of happiness herself.

Clearing her throat, she tried to bring the conversation back on track. "I get that you're frustrated, and yes, I'm happy to have you take over the bookkeeping. But please, follow Jen's advice." Veterinary work was often physically difficult, and as much as she felt crushed under the workload, she didn't want her father having a relapse, either. She'd have to talk to Jen and get the real prognosis, and if Dad was rushing things, she'd have a heart-to-heart talk with her mom. Her father might be bull-headed, but he would listen to his wife. Love had that effect on a man, or so she'd been told.

Cassie waited in the cool, casually decorated lobby of the Paradise Physical Therapy clinic, watching the minute hand tick its way around her watch. Stopping by without an appointment had been a mistake; it seemed the practice was much busier than she'd expected. It wasn't that she didn't have the time—Emma wasn't due to be picked up for another two hours and Mollie had cleared the rest of her appointments for the day—just that she hated waiting.

Flipping through an out-of-date magazine filled with celebrities she had never heard of, she wondered when she'd lost track of pop culture. Probably about the time she became a single mother. Between work and child-care, there hadn't been much time for movies or concerts, and her television habits had been reduced to educational cartoons. Although if half of what the magazines said was true, she hadn't missed much.

"Cassie?"

Her childhood friend looked the same as she had in high school, trim and athletic with curly brown hair pulled back in a neat ponytail. "Hi, Jen. Thanks for seeing me on such short notice."

"No problem. Thanks for waiting. Come on back. I'm going to grab some coffee in the break room before my next appointment."

Jen led her down the hall to a small but tidy room, then offered her a drink.

"Water would be great, thanks."

Jen handed her a bottle from the refrigerator, then poured a cup of coffee. "So what brings you by here? Is there a problem with your father?"

"No. Well, sort of. I'm just worried that he's pushing too fast. He says he's going to be back in the office in a week or two, and although I'd love the help, I'm afraid he's going to end up hurting himself worse."

Jen sipped her coffee. "I can't discuss his medical records with you. You know that. But I can say that, professionally, I don't see a problem with that plan. He'll be sore, but it shouldn't set his recovery back, if that's what you're worried about."

What felt like a hundred pounds of dead weight lifted from her shoulders. "Really? You think he's doing that well?" He'd been in such bad shape after the accident, it was hard to imagine him finally back at work. But she trusted Jen's opinion, so if she said he was up for it, then he was.

"Like I said, I can't release details, but since you are business partners, I can tell you the same thing I would put in a note for an employer. He's still got some hurdles to overcome, but yes, he should be clear for light duty in a few weeks if he feels up to returning."

"That's wonderful. Thank you, Jen. I know you're the reason he's done so well."

Jen dumped the last bit of her coffee in the sink and rinsed the cup. "I've done the best I could for him, but the truth is, your father is a strong man with an incredible work ethic. He gets full credit for his success."

Cassie laughed. "I think what you are trying to say is that he's tough and a bit bull-headed."

"You said it, not me," Jen replied, a grin on her face. "But really, it was good to see you. We should get together soon."

"I'd like that. Maybe once Dad is back up to speed, I can meet you for lunch or something."

"Sounds good. Just give me a call." Jen looked down at her watch. "Sorry to rush off so fast, but I've got another patient."

"No problem. I can see myself out." She gave Jen a quick hug goodbye, then navigated the twisting hallway back to the front lobby. Outside, the bright sunshine echoed her mood. Her father's recovery had been so long in coming, it was amazing to see the finish line after so many months of therapy.

"How come you never smile like that for me?"

Cassie startled, then saw it was just Alex, carrying a white prescription bag from the pharmacy next door. "Sorry, I didn't see you there."

"No apology needed. You just looked so happy I had to ask why."

"Well, I just talked with my father's physical therapist, and he's doing really well. In fact, he's going to be able to come back to work in a few weeks, if everything goes well."

"That's great news—in fact, how about I buy you a hot chocolate to celebrate?"

She did have a bit longer before she had to get Emma, and the only thing waiting for her back at the office was a stack of paperwork. She'd told herself Alex was off-limits, that getting involved was a bad idea. But it was just hot chocolate, not really a date. And when the choice was a sexy man with dimples to die for or writing up charts, there wasn't much of a decision to make.

"Hot chocolate sounds great."

Walking down Paradise's Main Street, she could feel everyone's eyes on her. They probably were wondering what she was doing with the new hot deputy when she hadn't been on a date in known memory. Small towns were great most of the time, but they didn't allow for much privacy. Luckily, the Sandcastle Bakery was only a few blocks away and served all sorts of hot beverages.

Inside the bakery, she stepped up to the glass display counter where Grace was sliding a tray of cinnamon scones onto a shelf. Normally, the pastries were a favorite of Cassie's, but right now she was too focused on the man beside her to care about food.

"Well, Cassie and Alex, what a surprise to see you two here…together." She winked at Cassie, no doubt remembering their earlier conversation about the good-looking deputy. "What can I get for you?"

"Two hot chocolates, please." Alex pulled out his wallet and paid for both, a move that had Grace raising an eyebrow in surprise.

"We're just celebrating Dad's recovery. Alex bumped into me as I was leaving the physical therapy clinic, and when I told him the good news, he suggested we come here."

"Well, that's very sweet of you, Alex." She handed him his change and then passed over the two cups, each with a hefty dollop of whipped cream on top. "You two have fun, now."

Alex held the door for her, and they walked back onto the sidewalk, Grace no doubt peeking out after them. This was why she didn't date. Well, one of the reasons why. The minute you said hello to a man, the entire town was all up in your business, watching your every move. She loved Paradise, but sometimes it felt like living in a reality show. Although having Alex as a costar in their own little romance was pretty tempting.

He was in khakis and a polo shirt today, looking strong and sharp and altogether too good for her. Not that he seemed to realize it. He hadn't taken his eyes off her since they ran into each other, his heated gaze warming her core faster than the hot drink in her hand. Desperate to change the subject, she tried to come up with a topic of conversation.

"So, my dad told me you need some help with Rex's training."

"We do. The department's been trying to find some volunteers. I guess the original plan was to have your father help, but even with all the progress your dad is making, I can't imagine he's going to be up to traipsing through the woods for quite a while."

"No, he's not." Again the guilty voice in her head reminded her that even though she'd been driving, her dad was the one in the brace. "But since he can't do it, I told him I would. Just tell me when and where you need me."

Alex stopped walking, his hot chocolate nearly sloshing over the side of the cup. "Really? You'd do that for me?"

"I'll do it for my father," she clarified. "I'm just filling in for him. That's all."

He grinned, his dimple winking at her. "Of course, and I appreciate it. Can you meet me at the wildlife refuge Saturday afternoon, around four o'clock?"

"I'll be there. Do I need to bring anything?"

"No, I'll have a pack for you and supplies. All you have to do is show up and enjoy yourself. It's really pretty straightforward."

Right. A day in the woods, purposely getting lost, while trying to avoid her growing feelings for a man she had no business falling for. What could possibly go wrong?

Chapter Seven

Alex ducked his head farther into his hooded sweatshirt. The relative warmth of the last week had broken this morning when a cold front blew in. Yesterday afternoon had been a balmy seventy-five degrees; today the mercury had stopped in the low forties and was expected to drop further at dusk. All over the island, people were putting sheets over prized rosebushes and bringing their potted plants indoors in advance of the expected freeze tonight. He'd thought about rescheduling the training session, but being able to work in all weather was part of the job description. Training only in perfect conditions wouldn't create a reliable dog, and with lives possibly in the balance, that was unacceptable.

"So tell me again. What do I have to do?" Mollie squinted up at him, shading her eyes from the bright but cool sunshine. She'd shown up with Cassie, a last-minute surprise volunteer. She seemed eager to work and hadn't complained once about the weather, which earned her points in his book. Right now, she was bouncing on the balls of her feet, waiting for instruction.

"You're going to wander away and find a place to hide. Spend about fifteen minutes or so walking before you stop. If you have any problems, you can use the radio, but otherwise try to keep quiet if you can. I want Rex to use his nose, not his ears."

"And he'll really be able to find me just by my scent?"

"That's the idea. He's going to be smelling the rafts of cells that fall off your body. Sometimes those fall right where your footsteps are, but sometimes they're blown around, pooling in invisible eddies of air. My job is to help interpret the wind patterns, as well as any terrain or temperature issues that might affect where the scent pools."

"I'm not sure if I'm fascinated or intimidated." Mollie's pixie-like features grinned up at him. "But I'm curious to see how well it works."

"Well, go hide, then, and we'll see how he does." Mollie gave a mock salute and started out across the scrubland that made up much of the Paradise Isle Wildlife Refuge. A few minutes later, she disappeared into a more densely wooded area shadowed by thick oaks.

With nothing to do but wait, he turned to Cassie, who'd been mostly silent since they arrived. "Sorry it's so cold out. I thought about canceling, but I'm not sure when my next day off is going to be, and Rex needs the practice."

"No, it's fine. I mean, you can't exactly choose the weather during a real search."

"Exactly. And I really want to get him up to speed. Police dogs don't usually do search and rescue, but with the nearest search group a few hours away, it makes sense to try to cross-train him."

"Really?" She cocked her head. "I thought all police dogs did that kind of thing—you know, tracking down bad guys and such?"

"Not all K-9s. And even then, not all scent work is the same. There's tracking, where they stay right along the footprints of the person they are following, and then there's air scenting, which is more what we are doing today. Rex will search in a zig-zag pattern to find the scent, then triangulate in. It's similar to how a police dog might clear a building. And then of course some dogs are also trained to detect drugs, or explosives, or even cadavers."

She shivered, and he had a feeling it wasn't from the cold this time. "That's kind of creepy."

"Well, sure. But at the same time, being able to provide closure for grieving families is pretty amazing."

"You're right. I'm sorry."

"No need. I'm just glad you came. Like I said, Rex needs the practice. He's doing well so far but hasn't made the jump yet to longer, aged tracks."

Cassie leaned down and ruffled Rex's fur. "I've got faith in you, buddy. You'll find her."

Energized by the attention, the dog bounced into a deep play bow, wiggling his butt in the air. "This cool weather has him acting like a puppy. We'd better let him burn off some energy while we're waiting or we won't be able to keep up with him on the trail." He pulled a tennis ball out of the backpack at his feet and tossed it to Cassie. "See if you can wear him out a bit while I double-check the map."

Cassie's face lit up at the challenge. She whipped the ball across the field and Rex tore after it as if it was the last ball on earth. Then, rather than waiting for him to bring it back, she chased after him, initiating a canine version of tag.

Crouched over his maps and log book, Alex couldn't help but notice how much more relaxed she seemed while playing with the dog.

"You should do that more often," he called out after watching them play for a while.

"Do what?" She walked back, the dog panting at her side.

"Smile."

Her back straightened stiffly. "Sorry, didn't realize I was such a downer usually."

Crap. "No, I just meant—well, you looked so happy just now. Not that you seem depressed otherwise, but you do seem a bit more weighed down most of the time." He shrugged a shoulder. "It was nice to see you just having fun. That's all."

"Oh." She bit her lip, an innocent act that had his mouth watering. "Well, I don't get a lot of time to just run and play. So thank you for inviting me out here."

"Hey, you're the one doing me a favor. But I'm glad you're not hating it."

She ducked her head. "Actually, I thought I would. In fact, I only agreed to help because my dad guilted me into it."

"Is it me? Have I done something to offend you? Or is it just the cop thing?"

"It's not you." She gave a wry grin. "I don't have a good relationship with the sheriff's department, that's all."

Well, at least it wasn't him; that was progress. "Anything I should know about? I'm too new to have heard much gossip, so I'd consider it a public service if you'd fill me in."

She smirked. "Public service? That's an interesting way to spin it."

Chuckling, he shouldered his pack. "We should get started now. And seriously, if it involves the department, I'd like to know, but if you're not comfortable sharing, that's fine, too. I didn't mean to put you on the spot."

She fell into step beside him. "It's not exactly a secret. I'm surprised you haven't heard all the details by now. I'll fill you in while Rex finds Mollie."

"If he finds Mollie. Remember, he's pretty new to this." He opened a small Ziploc bag that held a T-shirt of Mollie's and held it down for the dog to sniff. "Search, Rex. Search."

The dog snuffled the bag, then started sniffing around. Working back and forth in front of them, he covered an amazing amount of ground. Soon, his tail flagged up and he started moving in the direction Mollie had taken.

"Now what do we do?"

"Watch him and try to keep up."

Cassie watched the dog work, fascinated at the way he seemed to follow invisible signposts only he could see. Or, more accurately, smell. Alex was tracking each turn in his logbook, and he occasionally called out encouragingly to Rex. His love and pride in the dog and his dedication to his job were obvious. She respected that. And yet she'd treated him badly when they first met without provocation. He deserved to know why.

"Several months ago, my father and I attended a professional lecture over in Orlando. He drove on the way over, so I volunteered to drive home. It was late by the time we hit the Paradise Isle bridge, not much traffic at all. We were so close to home, and then, going through the intersection there at the base of the bridge, we were sideswiped. He didn't even slow down. I don't think he saw us at all, or the red light." She paused and turned to Alex. "The who that ran that light and hit us was an off-duty sheriff's deputy. He was drunk. He kept saying he was sorry over and over, and I could smell the booze on his breath. My dad had to be cut out of the car and still isn't back to work or able to walk without a brace. Jack, however, is just fine." Bile rose in her throat. "So yeah, I'm not a fan of cops right now."

Alex looked concerned, but to his credit he didn't exude sympathy like some people had. She hated pity.

"Jack? Jack Campbell? Older guy, real skinny?"

"Yeah, that's him. Paradise Isle's resident alcoholic. He was suspended, but because it was his first offense, he won't serve any jail time. His lawyer said he was a dedicated public servant going through a hard time, that it was a one-time mistake." Sarcasm coated her words. "No one is willing to acknowledge that he has a real problem. Least of all the Palmetto County Sheriff's Department."

"Wait, so you're saying the guys at the department are covering for him?" The disgust on his face made her like him even more.

"Maybe not covering for him exactly, but definitely

in some serious denial. Several of his friends accused me of exaggerating Jack's drinking, saying I was just trying to make trouble. Maybe they're right about it being the first time he's been caught, but given how frequently Jack closes down the only bar in town, I can't believe it was the first time he has driven under the influence. He needs more than just a slap on the wrist, but no one is willing to do anything about it. They act like I ruined his life, like he's the victim in all of this."

"Well, if it matters, I didn't know about any of it. I've been mainly working night shifts since I got here, so I'm a bit out of the loop."

It did matter. Reaching out, she squeezed his hand. "Thanks for listening, and thanks for believing me. I think that's been the worst part of this whole thing, having people not believe me."

He kept hold of her hand, tracing over her skin with this thumb. She shivered, and not from the cold.

"I do believe you. I'm not sure what I can do to help, but you can bet I'll keep my eyes open. Loyalty to fellow law enforcement is one thing, but I've been doing this long enough to know that not everyone lives up to the responsibility of the uniform. And when they screw up, they drag us all down with them."

His eyes had gone cold, as if locking down whatever pain that lesson had cost him. She could try to find out what had happened, but that seemed too personal just yet. Being here, walking hand in hand through the crisp air—that was enough for now.

Ahead of them the dog was getting more animated, making shorter zigs and zags as he narrowed in on the scent. The oaks were thicker here, the branches forming a living canopy of green above their heads. With the trees blocking some of the wind, it was quieter, the only sound the rustle of old leaves at their feet. It was hard to believe that this quiet oasis of green was only a few hundred yards from the beach and a short drive from the shops of downtown Paradise.

The quiet was broken by Rex's excited bark. "Sounds like he found her." He checked his watch and made a notation in his log. "Now he's supposed to make his way back to us so he can lead us to her."

At his hip, the radio crackled. "Hey, Rex was here, but then he ran off again."

Alex grinned, and spoke into the radio. "Yeah, he's supposed to do that. It's okay. He's coming to get us. We'll be there in a minute."

As he finished, Rex came bounding up, barking at Alex.

"I hear you. Bring me to her. Let's go." Alex broke into a jog behind the dog, and Cassie followed. The excitement of the moment was contagious; it was like being a kid on a scavenger hunt, racing to the next find. They crashed through some low-hanging branches and came into a clearing. Rex was waiting on the far side, getting petted by Mollie.

"Good boy, Rex. Good boy." Alex took a tug toy out of his bag and tossed to it Rex, who caught it in midair, then pranced around the clearing with it, shaking it gleefully.

"He's awfully proud of himself," Cassie commented, watching his antics.

Mollie stood and brushed the dirt from her jeans. "He should be. He did a great job. I didn't think it would be that quick."

"He was pretty incredible." Cassie had known in an

academic sense how amazing a dog's sense of scent was, but seeing it in action was another thing entirely. "Do you think he's up for another round?"

"I think so. He needs the practice, and he certainly doesn't seem tired." He handed her one of the printed maps. "Take this, just in case."

Cassie shoved the map into her pack, then patted the radio on her belt. "I'll take it, but if he doesn't find me, I'm calling for help. I can't navigate my way out of a paper bag without a GPS."

"Hey, I know. How about I go with you? I'm good with a map, and it will be more fun to hide together," Mollie suggested.

Alex quirked an eyebrow, but after a moment agreed. "I guess that would work. Lost hikers are often in pairs, so it would be worth trying. Just stay close to each other to keep from spreading the scent too far. Oh, and ladies?"

"Yes?" Mollie asked.

He winked. "No talking about me."

"What the heck was that about?" Cassie demanded as soon as they were out of earshot. "And don't give me that line about being good at reading a map. I've been on road trips with you, remember?" Mollie's sense of direction was even worse than her own.

"How else was I supposed to get a few minutes alone with you? So spill it. What's going on with you and Deputy Sexy-Pants?"

Cassie tried, and failed, to hold her laughter in. "You are awful. And nothing. Nothing is going on."

Mollie rolled her eyes. "Please. He can't keep his

eyes off you. And you keep checking him out when he isn't looking. Admit it. You think he's hot."

"What are you, twelve?"

Mollie grinned and stuck her tongue out at her. The girl had no shame.

"Fine, yes, I think he's attractive."

"Hot," Mollie corrected her.

"Okay, he's hot." There was no point in denying it; just the thought of his hard body and those bedroom eyes had her temperature rising. She grinned. "Total eye candy."

Mollie smiled in triumph. "And he likes dogs, rescues orphan kittens and is sweet to your kid." She ticked off each trait on her fingers. "In other words, perfect for you. You need to go for this."

Cassie shrugged. "I don't think there is anything to go for. I can't imagine he's looking to hook up with a ready-made family a few weeks after moving here."

Mollie rolled her eyes. "I'm not saying you have to marry the man. But you could go on a date or make out or something. Anything. Do you even remember how to kiss?"

"Mollie!" She smacked her friend on the arm. "And just when am I supposed to do this? While I'm covering my work and my father's at the clinic, or during the preparation for the charity dance, or maybe while I'm attempting to be both mother and father to a four-year-old girl?" It wasn't as if she hadn't thought about dating. But moving from the thinking stage to the action stage took time and energy. And it seemed as if there was never enough of either.

"You have friends and family to help with Emma.

And you weren't dating even before the accident, so it's not about that. Your real issue is that you're afraid."

She wanted to argue, but the truth was, she *was* afraid. Afraid of messing up again. Of falling for the wrong guy. Or worse, falling for the right guy and him not feeling the same way. As upset as she'd been when Tony left her, her heart hadn't been broken. He'd been an adventure, not the love of her life, and even then, it had still hurt. How much worse would it have been if she'd really had her heart on the line?

Annoyed, she tromped off through the leaves, angling east toward the ocean. Mollie stayed a few steps away. As they left the shade of the oaks, the landscape changed back to the saw palmettos and sand pines that were typical of the coastal scrub habitat. Picking her way through, Cassie made sure to avoid the sharp teeth of the saw palmettos, keeping an eye out for any other hazards. This area was home to a large number of native gopher tortoises, and stepping in a burrow would be a quick way to get a twisted ankle. They had walked almost to the edge of the boundary marked on Alex's map when she found a burnt-out log, the remnant of some long-ago brush fire. "This looks like as good a place as any to stop."

Resting against the damaged tree, she watched two bright blue scrub jays search for their evening meal as tension seeped from her shoulders. Her dad and Mollie were right; she had needed to get away from her responsibilities, at least for a few hours. And they were right about Alex, too, at least partly. He did seem like a good guy, and it wasn't right to lump him in with the likes of Jack Campbell. That didn't mean she was going to date him or anything like that. But maybe they could be friends, have some fun. What would be the harm in that?

Chapter Eight

Alex kept his focus, checking wind currents, watching Rex for signs of a find. But a part of his brain was stuck on how Cassie's hand had felt in his. He wanted to touch her again. Hell, he wanted to do a lot more than touch her. But she wasn't the type for a quick romp in the sack. And he didn't date women with children. Emma was ridiculously cute, but he knew he wasn't cut out for fatherhood. His own dad had failed spectacularly in that department and he had no desire to repeat those mistakes.

Growing up with a father more interested in his next score than his family had left its mark. He'd been ten before he gave up expecting his dad to show up at his Little League games or school parent nights.

He'd been twelve when his father went to jail for the first time.

His dad tried to say it was a bum rap, but the truth was, he'd been busted for possession. He'd sworn he'd get straight, and for about six months after his release, he did. Or at least, he'd seemed to. But then he started missing work and disappearing for days at a time. When the cops finally locked him up for good, Alex had been glad to see him go. Better no father than one who broke his promises as fast as he made them. Drugs or no drugs, he'd never been happy as a family man. He wanted more adventure than a wife and kids and mortgage could offer.

Alex had vowed never to be like him. He'd chosen law enforcement instead of a life of crime, but weren't those just two sides of the same coin? Working the streets of Miami was an adrenaline rush as addictive as any drug. Maybe he'd found a better way to channel his need for adventure, but that didn't mean he was any more suited to family life than his father had been. And unlike his dad, he wasn't willing to start one if he couldn't stick around for the long haul.

Which meant there was no way he could get involved with Cassie. "Look but don't touch" would be his motto.

He could do that. He would do that. He'd wanted to get more involved with the community, to let his guard down a little and make some real friends. Spending time with Cassie could be the first step in that direction.

Rapid barking broke him from his thoughts. Rex was just beyond the tree line, impatiently looking back at Alex as if annoyed with him for taking so long.

"I'm coming. Some of us only have two legs, you know." To pacify the dog, he eased into a run. Breaking through some low-hanging moss, he spotted the women up ahead. Mollie was taking photos of something with a camera she must have stashed in her pack, and Cassie was just standing there, waiting for him. Locking eyes with her, he felt energy crackling between them. Not daring to move closer, he stopped a few feet away.

"You found us," Cassie finally said, moving toward him.

"The dog did all the work." She was almost close enough to touch, but before he could make a move, Rex pushed into the space between them, nosing Alex for the tug toy he knew he'd earned. Nothing like a slobbery dog snout to cool off sexual tension. Tossing the toy to the dog, he marked down the details of the find, then took a swig of water.

"I think that's enough for today. If we stay out much longer, we'll be searching in the dark."

Cassie looked up from playing with Rex. "Can't he search in the dark?"

"Theoretically, yes. But we haven't practiced that yet, and I'd rather end on a high note and a successful find, just in case. When we move to night searches, I'll make it really easy for him at first, then gradually build to longer searches."

"That makes sense." Mollie chewed a granola bar, then stuck the wrapper in her pocket. "Besides, I'm hungry."

"You're always hungry," Cassie said. "It kills me that you can eat all day long and you never gain an ounce. I'm probably gaining weight just watching you eat."

"What can I say? Good genes, I guess."

Alex ignored the friendly banter. He'd learned long ago that there was nothing to be gained by entering into this kind of argument. Not that Cassie had any reason to be concerned. Her athletic curves were in perfect proportion. She must look amazing in a bikini.

Picturing her in one wasn't part of his "just friends" plan, and his body's quick reaction to the mental image was anything but platonic. Hoping to keep anyone from noticing his predicament, he turned to head back. He'd only made it a few steps when the chorus of "Cat Scratch Fever" blasted his ears. Turning, he saw Cassie grab her phone out of her pocket while shooting Mollie a dirty look.

"I change her ringtones every now and then," Mollie explained. "The last one was 'Who Let the Dogs Out.' Cassie isn't always as appreciative as she should be."

"What? When?" Cassie's face went white as she fired off questions. "Did you check under the beds? In the garage? The yard? Wait, what? Oh, my God." She sank to her knees, a look of pure pain on her face.

Crossing the ground between them in two strides, he took the phone from her limp hand. "Hello? This is Alex Santiago. What's the situation?"

He listened carefully. "We'll be right there, and I'll call for backup. Stay by the phone in case they need to reach you."

He turned to Mollie, who had an arm wrapped around her panicked friend. "It's Emma. She's missing."

Chapter Nine

Alex risked a glance at Cassie as he navigated the rapidly darkening streets of Paradise. She was staying strong, but he'd seen the tears that she'd silently wiped away. He couldn't imagine how frightened she must be. From what Cassie's father had told him, Emma had accidentally left the back door open and her kitten had escaped outside. They'd looked for it, but after an hour with no luck, the Marshalls had made Emma come in for dinner. Distraught over her pet, the little girl must have snuck back outside when she was supposed to be washing her hands.

Dr. Marshall wasn't mobile enough yet to do much searching, but Mrs. Marshall had searched the yard and house with no luck before calling Cassie. Their house backed up to the wildlife refuge with its acres of undeveloped land. The only good news was that the area he'd chosen for Rex's training session today was less than five miles from the Marshalls' neighborhood.

"I shouldn't have let her take the kitten with her," Cassie said.

"You had no way of knowing this would happen." They'd replayed this conversation several times already, but none of his assurances made a difference. Nothing would, other than finding her daughter, safe and sound.

A crackle of the radio pulled his attention back to the logistics of the situation. Backup was coming, but it would be a while. The deputy assigned to Paradise today was dealing with a serious traffic accident on the other side of the bridge and would be tied up for who knew how long. The main sheriff's office was almost an hour away, and the nearest trained search team was double that. Had the girl wandered off in the daytime he might not be so concerned, but given the remote location and the weather, he was calling in every person he could. In the meantime, he'd scour every inch of those woods himself if need be.

He pulled into the driveway only a few seconds ahead of Mollie, who was driving Cassie's car. Together they approached the house, where a large man with a cane was waiting on the porch. *He must be Cassie's father.*

Taking charge, he held out a hand. "Dr. Marshall, it's good to meet you finally. I'm sorry it's under such circumstances. Can we go inside?"

"Yes, sorry, come in." He led them through the door and back to the rear of the house into a large, comfortable kitchen. "I made some coffee. I didn't know what else to do. My wife's out looking for her, but I'm stuck in here with this damned leg like some kind of invalid." He slammed his cane on the ground, punctuating his words.

"I understand your frustration, sir, but trust me, you're going to be needed right here. First, I need you to get me something with Emma's scent on it. An article of clothing, a favorite stuffed animal—anything like that would work. While you're doing that, I'm going to take a look at my maps and maybe have some of that coffee you made."

The distraught man limped off toward another part of the house, the sound of his cane marking his progress. Alex wished he could offer more comfort, but the best thing he could do right now was work on finding Emma. Pulling out the maps he'd used during the training session, he located the Marshalls' neighborhood on the edge of the refuge. Marking it, he tried to figure out where Emma could have gone. The only road was the one they'd driven in on, and they had seen no sign of her. Which meant she most likely was somewhere in the refuge.

Cassie paced behind him, watching him work. She didn't ask any questions, probably because she was afraid of the answers.

Mollie shoved a cup of coffee in her hand, then placed one on the table next to the maps. A few minutes later, a sandwich joined it.

"Thanks." He took a bite and washed it down with the strong brew. When Cassie didn't join him, he looked up at her. "Eat. I can't afford you getting weak out there because you've got low blood sugar."

She looked as if she might argue, but Mollie steered her to the table and pushed her into a chair. Cassie picked at her food, but did seem to get some down. Good. There was no telling how long this was going to take; they all needed to be as strong and prepared as possible.

Dr. Marshall came back into the kitchen with a small stuffed bunny just as the back door opened. A tall woman with a noticeable resemblance to Cassie walked in, holding the missing kitten in her arms. "I found the cat, curled up in the shed, but Emma isn't anywhere." Her voice cracked. "I'm so sorry. I'm never going to forgive myself." Sobs shook her shoulders.

Cassie embraced her mother. "You didn't know. And we're going to find her. We have to find her."

Watching the two women cry was more than Alex could take. Shoving away the rest of his food, he stood and shouldered his pack. "Dr. Marshall, can I borrow that stuffed animal? And maybe a plastic bag to put it in?"

"Of course." He pulled out a bag from a cupboard, and placed the small, worn toy into it. "Here you go. It's her favorite. She's had it since she was a baby."

Alex could tell the man was trying to be strong for his family, but the strain was etched into the lines on his face. "Thank you, sir. I'm sure she'll be happy to have it when we find her."

Cassie let go of her mother. "You're going to have Rex search for her?"

He nodded grimly. "It's the best chance we have right now if we want to find her quickly. Once backup arrives, we can start a grid, cover more ground. But until then, with our limited manpower, I think it's our best option."

Mollie broke in, "But you said he wasn't ready for night searches. And Emma's been gone nearly an hour.

That's a lot longer than the tracks you had us making for him."

She was right, but there wasn't a better option. "I've been following the rule book with him, but he doesn't care about the rules. He does care about Emma. He'll do what he has to to find her."

Dear Lord, let that be the truth.

Cassie gripped a flashlight and waited on the back deck for the rest of the group. She'd stepped outside while Alex talked with the deputy team headed in their direction. It seemed the county search team was already deployed farther north and wouldn't be available until morning.

Acid swirled in her stomach at the thought of her little girl alone all night. She'd been wearing only a long-sleeve T-shirt and jeans, no jacket, when she snuck out. The weather was expected to drop below freezing in a matter of hours. Emma couldn't wait until morning. They had to find her now.

As if responding to her thoughts, Alex came through the French doors onto the patio, Rex at his side. Ignoring the hot tears burning her eyes, she knelt down and hugged the dog. "You have to find her, Rex. Please."

"Cassie, he'll find her. But we need to get started. The sooner we go, the easier it will be for him."

What he wasn't saying was that the odds were already stacked against them. Rex would be working a trail aged longer than any of the ones he'd practiced on and under new, nighttime conditions. Alex had assured her on the way over that search dogs worked just fine at night, but they both knew his lack of experience was working against them. He wasn't even a certified search-and-rescue dog, but he was all they had.

Alex opened the bag with Emma's toy in it and offered it to Rex to smell. The dog sniffed the toy, then started moving back and forth across the deck, his nose quivering. Instead of going down the steps to the yard, he circled back to the railing at the north side, where it met the house.

"That's where Emma likes to climb down from. She can reach the ground from that spot if she ducks under the rail." She started to scramble over the rail when Alex grabbed her arm.

"We'll take the stairs. He knows not to get too far ahead of us. He'll wait. And you won't be any good to your daughter if you end up with a sprained ankle."

Her face heated. He was right, of course. She took the stairs two at a time, needing to see what direction Rex was headed in. Alex's flashlight beam found the dog first, his reflective collar a beacon of hope. He was waiting at the edge of the yard, scenting the wind.

"The wind should make searching easier," Alex assured her.

And increase the risk of hypothermia. Damn it, what had Emma been thinking? The wildlife refuge took up almost half the island; there were a thousand places to get hurt or lost. "Emma!" Her voice lodged in her throat, her call coming out a raspy croak. Alex glanced at her, but kept his focus on the dog. Rex was moving quickly now, angling back and forth as he'd done in the training session earlier. In the distance, over the sounds of lovesick frogs, she could hear Mollie calling for Emma, as well. Mollie had chosen to walk the street, in case Emma had chosen to follow it. She'd knock on doors, as well, to get the neighbors in on the search. Everyone was doing what needed to be done. She needed to focus on that.

"Watch your step." Alex pointed to a broken branch she'd been about to trip over. "I know you're worried, but keep your head in the game."

She nodded. She would focus, for Emma's sake.

They were on an old walking trail, one that Cassie had taken many times in her life. Hopefully Emma had stuck to it. She'd be easier to find if she was on the path. "Do you think he knows where she went?"

"Definitely. See how high he's carrying his tail? He does that when he's got the scent."

Alex's confidence gave her the strength to start calling again. "Emma! Can you hear me, Emma? If you can hear me, say something, sweetie."

She strained her ears until she thought they would bleed, but there was no response. So she called again and again. Every step, every minute took an eternity.

"He's leaving the trail. You'll need to stay closer now, single file."

The dog had no trouble negotiating the thick press of wax myrtles and slash pines, but it was slow going for Cassie and Alex. Had her daughter really pushed through this kind of brush? "I can't believe Emma would have climbed through all this."

"She might have if she thought the kitten did. Or she could be on the other side of it. Remember, Rex isn't limited to following her exact path. He's scenting the air for her. He's going to take the shortest route to where she is right now."

Rex's shortcut had her arms covered in scratches, but she kept moving forward. At least in the trees it wasn't quite as cold. They trudged through for several minutes. Then suddenly they were back on the walking path again. Rex was picking up speed, his zig-zags getting tighter. Could he be narrowing in on her? Frantic, she called again. "Emma! Emma, it's Mommy. Can you hear me?"

Again, Rex veered off into the brush, this time angling down an embankment toward a creek that ran through this part of the refuge. Sliding down after him, she and Alex tried to keep up. "Wait, do you hear something?" Alex asked.

She paused, finding it hard to hear anything over the pounding of her heart. At first, there was nothing, but then she heard a whimper. "Emma?" Rex barked, then whined. Letting go of the root she'd been grasping, she slid down the rest of the way on her bottom. Alex was right behind her, his flashlight joining hers as they scanned the area.

There. Rex was nosing something on the ground a few feet away from the creek bank. Was it Emma? Dear God, were they too late? A sob ripped through her as she ran. Falling on her knees, she pushed the dog aside. There, curled up in the roots of an old oak, was Emma, white and motionless.

"Don't move her!" If the girl had any serious injuries, movement could make them worse. Cassie flinched at his words, but didn't pick her daughter up. Instead, she lay down in the mud beside her, murmuring something to her.

"Mommy?"

The child's voice sounded weak, but coherent. Thank God. As Cassie continued to soothe the girl, he swung his pack off his back and rummaged for an emergency blanket and the Thermos Mrs. Marshall had given him. "Here, put this on her."

Cassie tucked the flimsy metallic sheet over Emma, but the girl kicked at it, pushing into a sitting position. "Careful, honey, we need to make sure you're okay. Does anything hurt?"

"No. But I can't find Trouble. I looked and looked, and then I couldn't find me, either. I think we both got losted. Can Rex find Trouble like he found me?"

"Your grandma already found Trouble," Alex said. "He's waiting back at the house for you. I bet he's real worried about you." He placed a disposable thermometer strip on her forehead as he spoke and was relieved to see she was cold, but not yet hypothermic. "You're sure nothing hurts?"

She shivered, but shook her head. "My tummy's hungry. I didn't get any dinner."

Cassie hugged the girl, holding her tight. He could see the emotion in her eyes, but her voice was calm and upbeat. "I'm sure Grandma saved you a plate, but first we have to get you back up there. Can you walk?"

"I think so. I walked a really long time, but then my legs got tired and I sat down to take a rest."

"How about I give you a ride instead?" Alex could get her back to the house and medical attention faster if he carried her.

She nodded.

"All right. Why don't you have some of this hot chocolate your grandma sent while I call everyone and tell them you're okay? Then we'll all go back to the house and warm up. Oh, and here, your grandpa thought you might like this to keep you company." He handed her the stuffed rabbit he'd used for a scent article. Delighted, she snuggled the worn toy and curled up closer to her mother.

Satisfied the situation was in hand, he radioed in their status, then called Cassie's parents with his cell phone. They promised to relay the good news to Mollie and alert the neighbors, leaving him able to focus on getting Emma out of the woods, literally.

The cocoa seemed to have put a bit more color in her cheeks, the hot drink raising her spirits along with her body temperature. "You ready to go?" he asked her.

"Yes, please. I want to see Trouble."

Alex shook his head at the girl's tenacity. "All right, I'm going to pick you up, and you just hold on and enjoy the ride." Cassie helped the girl stand. Then he scooped Emma into his arms. She weighed nearly nothing, and he once again was reminded of what a close call she'd had.

Cassie led the way, using her flashlight to illuminate the path for both of them. This time, they stayed on the trail, trading the longer distance for easier going. Every so often, Cassie would lay a hand on Emma, as if to reassure herself the girl was safe. He didn't blame her. He was still shaken, and it wasn't his kid. Rex seemed to be the only one unaffected by the ordeal. He was enjoying the nighttime hike, sniffing trees and marking his territory. Just being a dog.

Cassie was watching him as well. "He gets free vet care for life. And anything else he wants. He's amazing."

"I think he wanted to find her as much as we did. He adores her."

"There they are!" Mollie's voice had Emma scrambling to get down. He tightened his grip. "Hold on there, sweetie, we're almost there."

They met up with Cassie's parents, Mollie and a paramedic team in the backyard.

"Is she okay?"

"She's fine, Dad, but you shouldn't be out here. You're not supposed to be doing stairs yet."

"Right here is exactly where I should be," her father replied gruffly, then planted a kiss on his granddaughter's head.

Cassie rolled her eyes, but Alex didn't blame the man. He must have been out of his mind not being able to help with the search.

"Just be careful going back up, okay?" Cassie asked.

"I will. You just get that girl inside and warmed up. I'll take my time, now that she's safe."

"You can all take your time," Alex said. "She's going to get checked out by the paramedics before anything else."

Emma spoke from his arms, still wrapped in the shiny emergency blanket. "What's a purple-medic?"

Cassie pointed to the waiting medic team. "These are paramedics. They're kind of like doctors, but they come to you instead of you having to go to Dr. Hall's office. They just want to give you a quick check-up."

Emma's eyes were wide, but she nodded. By the time Alex made it across the yard and up the steps, she was chatting about kittens with the medical team, winning them over with her charm. Inside, she proudly showed off a few new scratches, which turned out to be the extent of her injuries. Her body temperature was rising, as well, and the paramedics left her with a few neon bandages and instructions to drink lots of fluids and get a good night's sleep.

Once the paramedics were gone, everyone sat down to a late supper in the cozy country kitchen. Even Rex got his own plate of chicken stew. Emma cleaned her plate, but was rubbing her eyes by the end of the meal.

"I think I'd better get her home and into her bed," Cassie said, standing to clear her plate.

"Leave the dishes on the table. I'll get those later," Mrs. Marshall insisted. "And you don't have to go anywhere. You're welcome to spend the night here."

Cassie gave a weary smile. "I appreciate that. But honestly, I think we both need our own beds more than anything right now."

"I'll drive them home." Alex wasn't going to be satisfied until Emma was home, safe and sound. "And Mollie can bring you your car tomorrow sometime. The clinic is closed on Sundays, right?"

"Yes, but—"

"That's a great idea. You just give me a call tomorrow when you're ready for me to come over," Mollie gave her friend a hug, then left with Cassie's keys in her hand.

Alex said his own goodbyes, then escorted Cassie and Emma to the car. Mollie had left Emma's booster seat on the front porch, and he installed it in the backseat of his personal SUV, thankful he hadn't driven the department-issued vehicle today—there would have been nowhere for Emma to sit. "Your chariot awaits."

Giggling, the little girl let him buckle her in, her laughter a balm after the panic of the evening. For such a tiny thing, she stirred up big feelings, ones he didn't have a clue how to handle.

Chapter Ten

The drive home was a complete blur for Cassie. All she could think about was how close she'd come to losing her little girl. She tried to do all the right things, to live her life as carefully as possible, and yet she'd almost lost her daughter. Over and over in her mind, she saw Rex lying beside Emma on the cold ground. What if they hadn't gotten to her as soon as they had? What if Rex hadn't been trained so well? What if Alex had never moved to Paradise?

"We're here. I'll get Emma if you'll get the door."

Digging in her purse, she remembered Mollie had her keys. No matter. She kept an extra in a green ceramic frog by the front door. Retrieving it, she ignored Alex's raised eyebrow and opened the door for him.

"Remind me to discuss home security with you later," he whispered, carrying a sleeping Emma cradled in his arms.

She rolled her eyes, but knew he was right. One more thing to fix, to be responsible about. "Her room's down here." Keeping the lights off, she led him to the end of the short hall and into her daughter's pink-and-white room. Watching Alex gently lower Emma into her bed, as if he'd done it a thousand times, took her breath away. This simple moment was the kind of thing other families took for granted. Turning her back, she dug through the small white dresser for a nightgown. "I'll get her changed and be right out." She needed a minute to collect her thoughts, and she couldn't do that with him standing so close.

Once he left, she changed Emma out of the dirty clothes and into the clean nightgown. The exhausted girl never even stirred. Tucking the covers over her, she kissed her now warm forehead.

Alex was waiting in the living room, inspecting the various photos hanging on the walls. "She looks just like you did as a kid."

"Thanks. I think so, too. Listen, about tonight—"

"You don't have to say anything."

"Yes, I do. Emma means everything to me. If you hadn't been there, if we hadn't found her…" Her throat constricted, the sobs she'd been holding back finally breaking through.

Alex pulled her into his arms. "Hey, don't cry. I was there, and we did find her. She's going to be fine."

She sniffled. "What she's going to be is grounded for the rest of her life." With her head resting on his chest, she could feel his deep chuckle as well as hear it. "You think I'm kidding. I probably have a head of gray hair now."

He stroked her hair gently, caressing her. "Still looks as beautiful as ever," he whispered against her ear. Shivers of awareness danced across her skin, waking desires long buried. "I thought I was going to lose it out there. I don't know how you held it together."

"I had you." And that was the truth, she realized. He'd been there for her, giving her strength, making her stronger than she was on her own. Even now, she could feel the power radiating off him. Just once, she wanted to feel the full force of him.

Rising up on her toes, she looked at him, gave him a chance to pull away. When he didn't retreat, she pushed forward, taking his mouth with her own. He hesitated, then gave in with a moan, running his hands down her body, then back up again to tangle in her hair. He smelled like hot chocolate and pine trees and felt like heaven. Maybe this was wrong, but every fiber in her body was screaming for more.

She ran her hands up under his shirt, reveling in the hard planes of his body. Needing to see him, she tugged at the fabric, and he released her just long enough to strip it off. Panting, he rested his forehead on hers. "Are you sure this is what you want? Maybe I should go."

This was her out. Her chance to stop this madness and play it safe, by the book, the way she always did.

Screw that. Playing it safe hadn't kept her daughter from being lost or her dad from being injured. And it was one night. One night to break all the rules and just let herself feel. She deserved that. She needed that.

"Please, stay."

Alex had never been so turned on in his life. He'd tried to do the right thing; he'd given her a chance to kick him out. But no way was he strong enough to leave while she begged him to stay, not when she was tearing off his clothes and kissing him as if he was the last man on earth. He'd seen her fragile and upset; he'd seen her patient and gentle. Now he was seeing her passion, and it was more than he could take.

The most primal part of his brain wanted to take her right there on the living room floor. But with Emma in the house, that wasn't an option. Lifting Cassie, he carried her to the hallway. "Which room?" he managed to grunt as she rubbed against him.

"First door," she said in between nibbles on his neck.

He somehow made it to the bed, where they stripped each other in record time, barely stopping long enough for him to grab a condom from his wallet. Then Cassie was pulling him down on top of her, arching up to meet him. He tried to take things slowly, but she sped him on, urging him with her body to give more until they came together in one final moment of ecstasy.

Rolling, he pulled her against him while he tried to catch his breath. He could feel every heartbeat clear down to his toes, and instead of feeling spent, he felt more alive than he ever had before.

They shouldn't have done this, but he was glad they had. In fact, he didn't want to leave; he wanted to do it all over again. But he only had the one condom. Grabbing a tissue from the box on the nightstand, he went to dispose of it and froze.

"Um, Cassie?"

"Mmm-hmm?"

He tossed the offending latex in the trash and looked her in the eye. "The condom broke."

"Cassie, I'm so sorry. I've never had this happen before."

She had. Once. And the evidence was sleeping in

the room at the end of the hall. Alex reached out to brush her hair out of her face, and she jumped as if he'd burned her. She couldn't think when he was touching her. Pacing, she tried to comprehend what had just happened. Five years without sex, and this happens the first time she lets herself feel something? "Can you sit down so we can talk about this?" His voice was soothing, the way you might talk to a scared animal or child. But it didn't help.

"No, I'm trying to think. I pace when I think."

"Well, then, can you at least put some clothes on? Because I'm trying to think, too, and you're a bit distracting right now."

"What?"

He gestured at her still-naked body.

"Oh, yeah. Sorry." Turning her back, she grabbed a robe from the hook on the back of the door.

"No need to apologize, I was enjoying the view. We moved too quickly for me to get a good look before. You're gorgeous, you know."

"Thanks, but not helpful."

He sprawled out on the bed, making no move to cover his own nudity. Not that he should; his body was beyond impressive in every way. But unlike him, she was too worked up to be distracted by anything, even him.

"Is the timing…well…right? Do we need to be worried?"

She tried to do the math in her head. "I don't know. I need to get my phone." She crept out to the living room as quietly as possible. The last thing she needed right now was to wake up Emma. Her phone was in her purse in the middle of the floor. She took it and Alex's discarded shirt back to the bedroom, then pulled up her calendar app. "I think we're safe." She set the phone down and collapsed on the edge of the bed. She was going to be on edge until she got her period, no matter what the calendar said.

"I meant what I said. I've never had anything like this happen before. So you don't have to worry as far as diseases go. I'm healthy."

Her laugh was brittle. "Yeah, I'm healthy, too." If you didn't count the stress-induced heart attack she'd just almost had.

He put an arm around her shoulder, and she let herself lean against him. "So, are we good?"

She swallowed hard. "Yeah."

"Good enough to go again?" he teased, his hand stroking up and down her back.

She ignored the way her body reacted even through the thick robe and stood up. "I don't think that's a good idea."

He ran a hand through his sex-rumpled hair. "I know. I guess I should go, then."

"Probably." She tossed him his shirt and left him to dress.

She was waiting at the door when he came out. "Thank you again for finding Emma. And, well, everything."

He leaned down and planted a chaste kiss on her lips, igniting a slow burn that worked its way south. "Thank you for an amazing night. Sleep well."

She closed the door after him and leaned against the cool wood, hoping to douse the heat he'd raised. Sleep? He'd saved her daughter, rocked her world and then scared her to death in the space of one evening. She'd experienced more emotion tonight than she had in years.

Of course, he had no way of knowing that. He didn't have kids, didn't want kids, so although he'd been a rock tonight, he couldn't know how she'd felt. As for the sex, she very much doubted that was an unusual occurrence. He could have his pick of women in Paradise and probably did. He'd been too much of a gentleman to say so, but she knew a one-night stand when she saw one.

She still couldn't believe she'd attacked him like that. Her only excuse was the lingering trauma of nearly losing Emma. Her emotional control had been stretched too thin for too long, and he'd been around when it finally snapped. He'd been convenient, and she'd been overwhelmed. That was all.

Any other emotion she thought she felt could be chalked up to the drama of the night. She wasn't looking for a man, and he definitely wasn't looking for a family.

So why was she crying?

Chapter Eleven

The smell of coffee and frying bacon greeted Alex as he stepped into his mother's town house. She'd heard about the search last night and had called to invite him for breakfast. Mom's cooking or a bowl of cold cereal? He'd been half out the door before hanging up the phone.

"I'm in the kitchen," his mom called from the direction of all the good smells. "Make sure you wipe your feet."

Busted, he backed up a step and carefully wiped his shoes on the mat. All these years, and he still couldn't get away with anything when it came to her. Once he was sure he wouldn't track in any dirt, he found her standing over the stove. She set down her wooden spoon to give him a hug, then stopped and gave him a long, hard look. "So, who is she?"

"What are you talking about?"

"You tell me." She waved the spoon as she talked. "You've got that look on your face, the same look you had when you mooned over Rebecca Stutz in the sixth grade. And every girl since." She poured him a cup of coffee and handed it to him. "So, who is she? Is it that pretty animal doctor?"

He nearly choked on a mouthful of coffee. "How do you know about her?"

"What, you think you're the only one who can put a few clues together? Everyone knows. This is a small town, *mi hijo*. There are no secrets. So tell me about her."

"Sounds like you already know everything." She raised an eyebrow, and he capitulated. "She's great. Beautiful, smart, fun—"

"But?"

"But she has a daughter."

"And you don't like her little girl?" His mother's tone warned him he was on shaky ground. She'd been a single mother herself for many years.

"No, that's not it. Emma's a great kid. I really like her."

"So what's the problem? Is this doctor lady not a good mother?"

"Her name's Cassie. And she's a fantastic mother. She was beside herself last night when Emma was lost. She tries so hard to do the right thing by her girl. You'd really like her." She would, he realized. They were both strong women who'd made the best out of the hands they were dealt.

"But getting involved means I'd be involved with the daughter, too. And if the relationship progressed, I'd have to step into a role I can't fill. I don't have the first clue about how to be a father." He sat down on a stool and stared at the floor. "She deserves better."

"Please. There is no better. You are a good man, and you'll be a good husband and father someday. Not like—"

"But what if I am like him?" He stood, nearly knocking over the stool. "What if I'm exactly like him? I'm sure he didn't think that he'd turn out the way he did, that he'd put his own selfishness ahead of his family, but that's how it ended up. I'm used to being on my own, not having anyone to answer to. What if I can't change? What if I try, and then years from now, I can't handle it and I ruin their lives?"

His mother drew herself up and gave him the same look she'd given him when he brought home a bad grade in elementary school. "If you want something badly enough, you'll make it work. You always have. You've never been afraid of hard work, and a relationship is work like any other. It's all about putting in the time and effort. But only you know if it's worth it to you."

His mother's words made a kind of sense, but acid still boiled in his belly. She was his *mami*—of course she thought the best of him. If she was wrong, he'd be hurting innocent people.

Not that he'd been thinking about that last night. He hadn't been thinking at all. The minute Cassie had pressed her lips to his, he'd been working off pure instinct. Normally he trusted his instincts, but could he now?

His mother passed him a plate with bacon and eggs and put a tray of *mallorcas*, a sugar-topped pastry, on the table. The comforting smell awakened his appetite, and he dug in, chewing as he thought. There was no reason he had to make a decision right now. For all he knew, Cassie wasn't even interested in anything long-term.

"You think too much."

"What?" What kind of comment was that?

"You. You're thinking about everything that can go wrong from now until the day you die when you haven't even been on a date yet."

His face heated, and he shoved more food in his mouth, trying to avoid his mother's gaze.

"What? You've been out with her already?"

Damn. He swallowed carefully. "No, not exactly. But last night we spent some time together after all the excitement with Emma."

His mother narrowed her eyes at him. "I'm not going to ask because I don't think I want to know. But all the more reason you should take her out, do something nice. Behave like a gentleman."

"Yes, *Mami*."

"Now finish up so you can give me a ride to Mass. If we hurry, you'll have time for confession first."

This was why he usually avoided his mother's house on Sunday mornings. But darn it if the food wasn't worth it.

"Thanks for bringing me my car." Cassie swung into the driver's seat as Mollie scooted across to the passenger side. Emma was already buckled in in the back.

"No big deal. But I have to say, I'm surprised you're up so early. I thought you and Emma would sleep in after last night."

Cassie rubbed her eyes. "Yeah, I thought so, too. But

she was up at the crack of dawn, just like always. So since we were up, I figured we might as well be productive. We can pick up the rest of the decorations for the dance and be back in time for a nap. Hopefully."

"And you're okay with Emma going back to your parents' house so soon?"

"Honestly, Mom and Dad are as traumatized as anyone. They won't take their eyes off her for a minute. And seeing her bright-eyed and bushy-tailed will make them feel a bit better. We rushed out of there pretty quickly last night. Besides, taking Emma shopping for party supplies is like taking an alcoholic shopping for booze. She'd want to buy everything in sight."

"Whatever you say, boss."

They dropped Emma off with her grandparents, who were, as expected, eager to see she hadn't suffered any ill effects from her adventure the night before. And it seemed Emma wasn't the only one who'd gotten up with the sun. Cassie's father had already been to the hardware store and was installing small sensors on all the doors.

"These will alert us every time the door is opened and they'll keep buzzing if the door isn't shut all the way. She won't slip out unnoticed again."

Touched, she gave him a hard hug. "Thanks, Daddy."

He returned the hug, then spoke around the nail he had clenched in his teeth. "I've got another set of these for your house. Thought I'd drop by and install them when I'm done here."

"I'd love that. Thank you."

"Got to take care of my girls. Now, you and Mollie go shopping and don't worry about things here. You deserve a bit of fun."

Cassie turned away before her father could see her blush. She'd certainly had her share of fun last night, but she wasn't about to tell her father that. "Okay, I'll see you later. Bye."

She walked as quickly as she could to the car, then pulled out of the drive. As soon as they were on the road, heading to town, Mollie started in on her.

"So spill it. What happened with Deputy Sexy-Pants last night?"

She coughed, trying not to laugh. "What makes you think anything happened?"

Mollie rolled her eyes. "Because you know better than to wake me up this early just to go shopping. So there must be something you're dying to tell. So tell me everything, and include lots of detail."

She couldn't stop the grin she felt splitting her face. "You mean, besides sleeping with him?"

"What?" Mollie shrieked. "You had sex with him? Last night? I thought you'd maybe made out, a good-night kiss, that kind of thing."

"Well, we did that, too."

"Who cares about that now? Go back to the sleeping together part. Is he as gorgeous naked as I think he is?"

She thought of his hard, tanned body and nodded. "Oh, yeah."

"So does this mean you guys are dating, or what?"

"I don't know. I don't think so. I mean, we didn't discuss it. Things got a bit complicated, and then he left."

"Huh? I mean, it's been a while since I've engaged in that particular activity, but I don't remember it being very complicated."

Cassie eased into a parking space behind the stationery and party goods store. Turning off the car, she stared out the window. "The condom broke."

"Are you kidding me?"

She covered her face with her hands. "I know. I still can't believe it. One minute I'm coming on to him, and the next I'm pacing the room, panicking that I'm pregnant."

"Well, are you?"

"I don't think so. I'm pretty sure the timing wasn't right."

"Wait, did you say you came on to him?"

"I totally did. I didn't even know I had it in me, but hell, Mollie. I've spent so long trying to do everything right, and bad stuff still happens. I figured I might as well do something I wanted to do for a change. So I went for it."

"Well, good for you. I mean, not for the whole birth-control fiasco, but still, it's nice to know you still have some life in you. But what are you going to do now?"

"I have absolutely no idea."

"Well, I do. We're going to shop. I don't mean just party stuff. This kind of news calls for at least a new pair of shoes, if not a whole new outfit. Actually…" she said, tapping her fingers on the door handle. "We can look for a new dress for you to wear to the dance. Something that will knock his socks off. When I'm through with you, he won't know what hit him."

Cassie sipped carefully at her hot tea and eyed the pile of bags and packages on the coffee shop chair beside her. Had she really bought all of that? They'd probably still have been shopping if she hadn't distracted Mollie with the promise of caffeine and baked goods.

She wiggled the shoe box out of the stack and snuck a peek under the lid again. "I'm going to break my neck walking in these."

Mollie set down her café con leche and broke open a chocolate-filled croissant. "No, but Alex might, tripping over his tongue when he sees you."

The sharp-heeled shoes were higher than any others Cassie owned, but they were incredibly sexy. As was the dress Mollie had talked her into. And the lingerie that was so barely there she'd blushed when the checkout girl rang it up, much to Mollie's amusement. She didn't even know why she'd bought it. She wasn't planning on a repeat of last night—was she?

"So when do you think you'll see him again?"

"I honestly don't know. I guess at the dance, if not before."

"That's almost two weeks from now. You've got to see him before that! You should call him."

"And say what, exactly? 'Thanks for the most passionate night of my life. Were you interested in having coffee sometime?'"

"Most passionate night? You cannot let this guy get away. If you won't do it for yourself, do it for all of us who barely remember what a good man is like."

"You really think I should go for it?" She wanted to believe that he *was* a good man, but she'd been wrong before. Really, really wrong.

Mollie straightened in her chair, a devilish look in her eye. "I definitely do. And I take it back. You don't have to call him."

"What? Why not?"

"Because he just walked in."

She turned, and sure enough, there he was. Heart

pounding, she ate him up with her eyes. He was wearing snug jeans and a black T-shirt, the uniform of bad boys everywhere. But he was one of the good guys. He'd proved that to her, over and over. So why was she so scared?

"Hey, Alex, over here." Mollie waved him over with all the subtlety of a Great Dane. She wasn't afraid of anything.

"Hey, Mollie." His gaze shifted to Cassie. "Hello, Cassie. How are you?"

"I'm good." Good? That was her version of witty conversation?

He smiled, that long, slow smile that made his eyes crinkle just a bit and brought out his dimples. "I'm good, too. Great, actually, now that I've seen you. I was going to call you when I got home, but this is even better."

Mollie pulled out a chair for him. "Have a seat."

"Well, I was going to get some coffee—"

"I'll get it. My treat. You and Cassie sit and chat."

As if realizing he had no choice in the matter, he sat down and watched Mollie dart to the counter to place an order. "So she knows, huh?"

Cassie chewed her lip. "Well."

He placed a hand on hers where it rested on the table. "I'm not mad. In fact, I might be a bit flattered."

"Flattered?" That was much better than angry.

"Well, I figure, if you thought it was awful, you might be too embarrassed to share."

His thumb was tracing little patterns across her skin, short-circuiting her brain. Mollie saved her from responding by plunking down a coffee cup next to their joined hands.

"Well, aren't you two cute."

Cassie smacked her with her free hand.

"What? You are. Anyway, you two enjoy. I'm going to run over to the library and pick up some books I reserved. Whenever you're done, you can just pick me up over there. Bye-bye." She breezed out with a wink, bumping the pile of bags as she went.

Alex grabbed them, but not before several of them spilled their contents to the floor. Of course, the lingerie box had ended up on top, the store name emblazoned on the lid for anyone to see. He tapped a finger on it. "So, doing some shopping, I see."

Her face was on fire. She might actually die of embarrassment right here in the town coffee shop.

He grinned, then put everything back in the bags. "Sorry, but you're driving me crazy here."

"I am?" She was?

"Yeah." His deep voice sent flickers of awareness down her spine. "But I also know that we kind of got things out of order, and I'd like to make up for that, if I can."

"Out of order?" Had she messed something up last night? It had been so long since she'd had sex, maybe she'd done something wrong.

"Yeah, I realized that we haven't actually been out on a date. And I'd very much like to take you out and get to know you a bit. What do you think?"

"What about Emma?" Damn it, she hadn't meant to blurt that out. "I mean, does it bother you that I have a child?"

His face turned serious, and he ran a hand through his hair. "I'll be honest. If you'd asked me that a month ago, I would have said yes. But Emma's a great kid. Of course, it probably helps that she's out of the diaper stage. Anyway, what I'm trying to say is, I'm not willing to walk away from whatever's happening between us. I don't think I can."

Alex waited, his heart pounding, for Cassie to say something, anything. He'd taken a chance; now it was up to her. He couldn't take it back now—and he didn't want to take it back. But if she wasn't willing to try, there was nothing he could do.

"What did you have in mind? As far as a date, I mean."

He let out the breath he'd been holding and resisted the urge to kiss her. He'd said he wanted to take things slowly, and he meant it. At least, he did when he wasn't actually this close to her, smelling the mango-scented body lotion she wore. Reeling in his libido, he focused on her question. "I was thinking dinner, Friday night. How does that sound?"

She nodded. "I'll get someone to watch Emma."

"I'll pick you up at seven?"

"That sounds perfect." She gathered up her packages and stood. "I really should get going, but I guess I'll see you Friday."

"You can count on it." He got the door for her, then took his coffee and strolled back to his car. Grabbing one of the *mallorcas* out of the bag on the front seat, he munched it while sipping the strong brew. Rex raised his head hopefully. "Sorry, buddy, these are for people only." The big dog sighed and lay back down on his blanket, content to snooze through their shift. At least one of them would be caught up on sleep.

Not that he was complaining. Every moment spent with Cassie last night had been amazing. He only wished they'd had more time together. Once with her was definitely not enough. He'd lain awake the rest of the night, his body unwilling to calm down. He hadn't felt this worked up since he was a teenager. And seeing those lingerie boxes hadn't helped.

Cassie in lingerie wasn't something he should be thinking about if he wanted to keep his promise about starting over and moving more slowly. Jumping into the deep end had made his hormones happy, but that kind of plan wasn't fair to Cassie or her daughter. He was venturing into unknown territory, so slow and steady was the way to go. Until he knew he could make things work, he needed to keep himself under control.

Checking traffic, he pulled out onto the street carefully. Sunday afternoon was a busy time for downtown Paradise, with the after-church crowd hitting the shops and restaurants before heading home. Families of various sizes strolled up and down the sidewalks, giving him a good view of what his future might look like if he and Cassie ended up together.

Watching a man with a toddler on his shoulders, he wondered if his own father had ever done anything like that. He certainly didn't remember any father-son outings. All of his memories were of disappointments and broken promises. He'd die before he'd put Emma through that kind of pain.

But for the first time, he found himself wondering what it would be like to be one of the good fathers. To have someone look up to him, want to be like him. Would he be strengthened by that kind of love? Or would he feel stifled by the responsibility, the way his father had? Being a parent meant being there all the time, forever. He'd never even managed to keep a plant alive for more than a month, let alone commit to a human for the long haul. Maybe he didn't have what it took. But the way he felt about Cassie, and Emma, made him wish he did. Maybe that was enough for a first step.

For now, he needed to keep his mind on work. He was due in for a staff briefing at the top of the hour, and the chief deputy had asked to speak to him afterward. Luckily the Paradise Isle substation was only a mile away from the café. He was able to park, change and make it to the conference room with time to spare. The meeting itself was uneventful, mostly covering the new forms the county had started requiring and a reminder about the free bike helmet program now in place. Deputies were to keep a few in their vehicles to hand out if they saw a child violating the helmet law. Alex had already handed out several since he'd started the job. He'd rather hand out helmets than tickets any day.

Meetings like this used to bore the heck out of him. He'd never seen a need to sit around talking about things when he could be out actually doing something. But lately he'd found himself looking forward to the briefings. The information he gained made him more effective when he was out on patrol, and he liked having a view into the big picture. Funny how a bit of time and experience could change your perspective. Maybe there was hope for him yet.

Chapter Twelve

Cassie stripped off her dress and threw it on the bed with the other five she'd tried and discarded. A knock at the door had her scrambling for her robe. "I'm coming." With her luck, Alex was here early, and would find her half-naked with no babysitter. Holding the terrycloth together, she peered through the peephole.

It was Mollie, thank heavens. Turning the lock, she let her in.

"I got your message and came right over." She eyed Cassie's ugly orange robe. "And none too soon. Shouldn't you be dressed by now?"

"Yes, and I would be, but Mom canceling kind of threw off my schedule."

"Is she okay?"

"She will be. It's just strep throat. But she's contagious until she's been on the antibiotics a few days, so—"

"So I'm here to save the day. No problem. Emma's

easy. You're the difficult one. Have you even picked out what you're going to wear?"

She thought of her torn-apart closet and winced. "Not exactly."

"And when is he picking you up?"

She checked the clock. "Any minute."

"Well, I'm hardly one to give fashion advice, but I'm pretty sure anything would look better than that robe."

She had a solid point. "Emma's—"

"Emma's handled. I'll make her some dinner, and then we'll watch movies and drink hot chocolate. Don't worry about her. Just go take that thing off before your Prince Charming shows up and thinks you've turned into a pumpkin."

Mollie always did have a way with words. Retreating into the bedroom, she heard Emma's squealed greeting for her favorite babysitter. Gratified that her daughter would have a good night, she braved the closet again. It would help if she knew where they were going to eat, but Alex hadn't said when he'd left her a message confirming the date, and she hadn't had a chance to call and ask. More to the point, her stomach had clenched up in nervous knots every time she thought about picking up the phone to call him. Which was ridiculous; she wasn't an awkward teenager anymore. There was no reason to be nervous about a simple date.

And no reason to be so worked up over what to wear. Telling herself to stop acting like a lovesick schoolgirl, she chose a simple but attractive sweater and a black pencil skirt. A pair of strappy black heels that she'd purchased on a whim last year finished the outfit.

She'd just finished her makeup when Mollie poked her head in the room. "He's here. And he's gorgeous.

If you don't hurry up, I'm going to go out with him myself."

"I'll be right out." Luckily her hair didn't require much work. A quick brushing and she was as ready as she was going to get.

In the living room, she found Alex sitting on the floor, coloring with Emma. Relaxed, lounging in her living room with her daughter, he looked like a dream come true. What would it be like to have this kind of scene every night?

Whoa. Tonight was about dinner, not happily-ever-after. She was going to scare him off before they got out the door. "Sorry you had to wait."

He looked up and grinned. "No problem. Emma was an excellent hostess. She even gave me first pick of the coloring books."

Those dimples were going to be the death of her. "I'm happy to hear it."

Mollie came in, licking a wooden spoon. "Mac and cheese is ready, so I'm going to steal my dinner date away from you folks."

Emma jumped up, nearly knocking over the crayons in her excitement for her favorite meal. "Bye, Mom. Bye, Deputy Alex." Whizzing past, she raced into the kitchen.

"Well, I guess she's okay with you leaving, huh?"

Cassie shrugged. "I guess so. Although a kiss good-bye might have been nice." She grabbed her purse and checked that she had her cell phone and keys. "So where are we going?"

"Actually, that's up to you."

"Um, okay."

"You have two options. If you're up for it, I'd love to make you dinner at my house. I picked up some food and wine, and I am fairly certain I won't set the house on fire. But if you'd be more comfortable, we could go out. I've got reservations at Isle Bistro, just in case."

He cooked? She wanted to say yes to that, but could she trust herself to be alone with him? The restaurant was a safer choice, but it would be loud and crowded on a Friday night. Not exactly the best atmosphere to get to know each other.

"If you do let me cook for you, I want to be clear— it's just dinner. I'm not trying to trick you into anything else."

She believed him. That he'd thought to give her another option showed he wasn't trying to manipulate her into something. Besides, she was dying to see what he could do in the kitchen—no guy had ever made her a meal before. "You're really going to cook?"

"Absolutely."

"Well, let's go, then."

Yelling a goodbye to Mollie and Emma, she followed him out to his car, where he held the door and offered a hand to help her climb up. Ignoring the thrill of awareness that his touch sparked, she settled into the SUV. How was she going to survive an entire evening with him if just the touch of his hand got her all worked up? And why did he have to smell so good?

"Are you okay over there?"

She realized she was gripping the seatbelt like a lifeline and relaxed her hands. "Fine."

"You know, I meant what I said. I'm not trying to seduce you or anything. I don't want you to be worried about my intentions for tonight."

"No, I trust you." And she did. She was the one she didn't trust.

* * *

Alex parked in front of his apartment. He'd chosen a ground-floor unit that had a small yard in a newer building just a block off Main Street. He'd barely opened the door before Rex barreled into him. Spotting Cassie, the big dog darted off, returning to drop a rather damp tennis ball at her feet. "Sorry, big guy, but I don't think you're supposed to play ball in the house."

"Definitely not. He knocked over a lamp the last time."

She gave the disappointed dog a scratch. "Can I help you in the kitchen?"

"No need. I already made the salad, and everything else is going right on the grill."

"The grill. I should have known. Somehow I couldn't picture you standing over a hot stove."

"Grilling counts as cooking." At least he hoped it did, because she was right—he wasn't much use in the kitchen otherwise.

"I suppose it does. Besides, I'm too hungry to argue."

He was hungry, too, but not the way she meant. He'd been trying not to stare since he picked her up. She was sexier in her ladylike skirt and sweater than any bikini-clad beach bunny. Tearing his eyes away before his body betrayed the direction of his thoughts, he opened the refrigerator and found the platters he'd made up earlier.

"Can I help carry something out, at least?" She'd followed him into the tiny kitchen, unaware of the effect she had on him.

"You could bring the wine. It's on the counter by the stove." Hefting the trays of meat, he let her open the door to the patio. "While the grill heats up, I'll get the table ready. You just sit and relax."

Inside, he found the plates and silverware, and a stack of cloth napkins he didn't remember buying. Stacking everything up, he grabbed the salad bowl with his free hand and headed back outside.

He'd expected Cassie to be sitting at the table sipping her wine. Instead, she was out in the yard, playing tug of war with Rex. She'd kicked off her shoes and was barefoot, laughing in the grass. And she was beautiful.

She saw him and paused. "I hope you don't mind. He really wanted to play."

Mind? He couldn't think of anything he wanted more than to see her laughing and happy like she was right now. "Of course not. Have fun. I'll let you know when the food's ready."

Loading up the grill, he watched her play in the moonlight. He'd never met anyone like her. She was dedicated and driven, and if he hadn't looked closely, it would have been easy to think that's all she was. But he'd seen the softer side, the playful side that he had a feeling she didn't often let show. He admired how seriously she took her work and family responsibilities, but everyone needed some downtime. He had a feeling she didn't allow herself nearly enough of it.

He was just turning off the grill when she came back and collapsed into a chair.

"I hope you worked up an appetite out there. The food's ready."

Reaching for the wine glass he'd filled for her, she took a sip. "Perfect. I'll just go wash up."

"Past the living room, first door on the right."

"Thanks."

He had the food on the table when she returned. "Wow, that looks amazing."

"So do you."

She blushed at the simple compliment. He got the feeling she wasn't in the habit of hearing them. Obviously, she'd had at least one prior relationship, but maybe she wasn't as experienced as he'd thought. One more reason to back up and slow down. And maybe do some damage control while he was at it. "Listen, about the other night. I want to apologize."

She looked up, eyes wide. "Apologize?"

He rubbed the back of his neck. "Yes, apologize. I shouldn't have taken advantage of the situation. You were vulnerable, and I should have realized that."

She crossed her arms against her chest, and her chin jutted up. "You know, I'm a grown woman, and I make my own decisions. I don't need you to look out for me."

"No, I didn't mean it that way. But I also don't want to be a reason you look back and regret anything."

She paused, her fork midway to her mouth. "Do you regret it?"

"Absolutely not."

Her face relaxed. "Good. Me, either."

Time to change the subject. "It was good to see Emma so happy today, after everything."

Cassie swallowed and nodded. "She's bounced back like nothing ever happened. Out of all of us, I'm pretty sure she's the least traumatized."

"She's a lucky girl to have so many people who care about her."

"She does have that. My parents are nuts about her, obviously. And Jillian and Mollie both help out when I need them to. They're great friends, and Emma's really comfortable with them."

"What about her father. Does he spend much time with her?"

Her lips pressed together in a hard line.

"I'm sorry. If that was too personal a question…"

"No, it's fine. I'm actually surprised you hadn't heard the whole sad story already."

"I'm new in town, remember?"

"True, but once people find out you're interested in me, it will come up. Trust me."

"Well, if that's the case, it's probably better I hear it from you."

Cassie folded and then refolded her napkin, finally setting it down next to her plate. "I met Tony right after I graduated from veterinary school. I'd spent the last months—years, really—working my butt off, and I thought I'd earned a bit of fun. So I went with some girlfriends on a gambling cruise, one of those boats that goes out into international waters for a few hours."

He nodded. "A booze cruise."

"Yeah, basically. Tony was there with some buddies and we kind of hooked up. He was older and a first mate on a yacht docked in Port Canaveral. He was fun and so completely different from anyone I knew. Later he took me dancing, and to clubs, all the things I'd missed out on holed up in my room with my books." Picking up her glass, she drained the last of the crisp wine. "I thought he loved me. Even so, we were careful, except for the first time. But you know what they say. It only takes once." At the tightening in his jaw, she said a silent prayer that history wasn't going to repeat itself. "Anyway, when I found out I was pregnant, I still thought everything would be okay. I was about to start work at the clinic, he had a decent job, and we'd have our own little family." Looking back it was hard to believe she'd ever been that naive. "As I'm sure you can imagine, he had a very different reaction."

"Was he angry?"

"Not exactly. He just said he needed some time to think about it. That was about five years ago. I haven't seen him since."

"What? What happened to him?"

She shrugged and started stacking the plates. "Last I heard, he was in the Bahamas. He had some friends who worked boats down there. Honestly, I haven't tried too hard to track him down. Let sleeping dogs lie and all that."

Alex took the plates from her hand, setting them back down with a *thunk*. "But what about child support? Even if he doesn't want to stick around, he could still be sending money."

"The money isn't worth it. If I tracked him down, made him pay, he might fight me on custody. As far as I'm concerned, he lost out on that chance when he left, and I'm not going to let him come back and screw up her life. I've seen what that does to kids—having dads who come and go, breaking promises, forgetting birthdays. I'm not going to put Emma through that, not over money. Having no father must be better than having one who doesn't really care."

Chapter Thirteen

Alex thought about all the times his dad had left him waiting, all the baseball games he'd been too drunk to remember, the school award ceremonies he didn't bother to show up for. Alex's heart had been broken more times than he could remember, and he had the emotional scars to prove it. "You're right. Nothing's worse than waiting for a parent who never shows up."

She sniffed and nodded. "So you see why I have to be careful. I can't mess up like that again."

His head spun. "Wait, what? How is this your fault? He's the one who ran out. That's all on him."

"But I let it happen. I went out with him. I believed him. I went to bed with him. If I'd been smarter—"

"Stop it." He took her by the shoulders. "You were young, and maybe you made a mistake. Guess what? Everyone makes mistakes. The difference is, you did everything you could to make things right. You've been an amazing parent to that little girl, and that's what counts. He could have done the same. Hell, even if he didn't want to stick around, he could have at least made an effort to help support you and the baby financially." He looked her in the eyes. "Don't blame yourself for his failings."

He wanted to kiss her until she believed what he was saying. He wanted it so much that he let go and took a step back. So this was why she'd looked so upset when Jillian and Mrs. Rosenberg had been talking about proud fathers handing out cigars. This Tony person certainly hadn't stuck around to celebrate or do anything else, for that matter. Angry at a man he'd never met, he worked to calm himself. Getting upset wasn't going to help anyone, least of all Cassie.

Calling Rex over, he stroked the dog's soft fur, feeling the tension seep away. "Your Tony sounds a lot like my dad. Lots of fun, but not someone you can count on when things get tough. The difference is, my father stuck around, at least for a while. He'd hold down a job, pay a few bills, buy a few groceries, then get fired for coming in drunk or not showing up at all. Even when he was working, he was more likely to spend his paycheck on drugs than pay the rent. We moved around a lot until my sister was old enough for school and Mom could get a job. Things got better when she stopped relying on him for anything."

"Oh, Alex, I'm so sorry. That had to be so hard."

"It wasn't great. By the time I was in middle school, he was pretty bad off. He went from using to selling and got busted."

"He's in jail?"

"I don't know. Probably. He's been in and out so many times, he probably has a cell named after him. I stopped keeping track years ago."

"Is he why you volunteered for the mentor program?"

"I guess, yeah. I know what it's like to grow up without a man around to look up to. And I know how easy it is to head in the wrong direction. I had a teacher who took an interest in me, got me thinking about college instead of easy money. Otherwise, I could have ended up just like my old man."

Cassie came over to where he stood and wrapped her arms around his waist. Tipping her head back, she met his gaze. "But you didn't. You're hardworking, dedicated and caring."

"You forgot sexy."

Her eyes twinkled up at him. "That goes without saying."

This time he was the one to initiate the kiss, capturing her mouth the way he'd wanted to all night. Her lips were warm, her tongue hot as she opened for him. Pulling her against him, he forced himself to go slowly, to draw every second of enjoyment out of this. It would be so easy to pull up her skirt and take her right there on the patio. The little moans she made told him she wouldn't tell him no. But he'd made a promise. Holding himself in check, he gentled the kiss, smoothing her hair with his hands to soothe himself as much as her. Sensing the shift, she pulled away and looked up at him, questioning.

"If we don't stop now, I'm not going to be able to stop." Just watching her, with her lips swollen and her cheeks flushed, made him want to pick her up and cart her off to his room. But after what she'd been through with her ex, that wasn't an option. He needed to prove to her he wasn't going to turn and run when the going got tough. Hell, he needed to prove it to himself, too. Until then, he had to keep things from getting too intense too fast. And sex with Cassie was nothing if not intense.

She swallowed, understanding showing in her eyes. "So, now what?"

"How about a drive before I take you home?" At the mention of a drive, Rex came bounding over, nearly tap dancing in his excitement.

Cassie laughed. "Rex certainly thinks it's a good idea. And I do, too. A drive would be nice."

He took the dishes into the house, leaving them in the sink for later. At the front door, Rex waited impatiently, his leash in his mouth. Alex never should have taught him that trick. "You know, I don't have to bring the dog along. He'll be fine here."

"Oh, bring him. I'm sure he's used to going everywhere with you."

Outnumbered, he snapped the leash on Rex. "Fine, you can come. But she gets to ride shotgun."

"Mommy, I'm bored." Emma's pouting had started within minutes of her arrival at the clinic and was giving Cassie an epic headache.

"Honey, I'm sorry, but we can't go home yet. I've got a patient coming in later, and I have to finish up some paperwork."

"Then I wanna go to Grandma's house like I always do."

Cassie sighed. Emma was usually so good, but today she was really out of sorts. Her dad had what was hopefully his final visit with the orthopedist today, and her mom had wanted to be there to ask some questions. Once her father was back at work, Cassie could spend more time with Emma in the afternoons, but until then Emma was just going to have to cope. They all were.

"Do you have any puppies or kittens for me to play with today?"

"Honey, I already told you we don't. I know. Why don't we go up front and get some paper and crayons, and you can color for a while?"

"I guess." Emma started down the hall, scuffing her feet. It really was pretty boring at the clinic today. Normally there were clients in and out who would show Emma some attention or pets to play with. Today was slower than normal, and even Cassie felt a bit restless. The weather outside wasn't helping, either. Today was the first day of really warm weather and everyone had a bit of spring fever.

"Mommy! Come look. Rex is here!"

Rex? He didn't have an appointment; she'd just checked the schedule a few minutes ago. Coming around the corner, she saw Mollie tossing Rex a treat, the phone at her ear, and Alex leaning on the counter, looking exactly like a man in uniform should look.

"Is Rex okay?"

"He's fine, just a bit bored. I thought we'd stop in and pick up a few of those dental treats you told me about and pay a visit to a pretty lady." He looked down at Emma and smiled. "Seems we got a two-for-one deal on that."

Relieved there was nothing wrong, she ran a hand through her hair, trying to smooth it. It was always a mess by this time of day. "How have you been?" It had been a few days since their dinner, and she had missed him more than she'd expected. Not that she thought he'd been avoiding her, but they both had busy schedules that didn't seem to overlap much.

"I'm good. Better now that I've seen you. I hope you're ready for the dance this weekend?"

She felt her cheeks warm. "Definitely."

"That's good because I'm looking forward to dancing with a particular volunteer."

Emma looked up from playing with Rex, her eyes wide. "Are you taking Mommy and me to the dance?"

"Oh, no, honey, Alex didn't mean—"

"I'd be honored to escort you and your mother to the dance." He winked at Cassie. "In fact, that's really why I stopped by. To formally invite you to be my dates."

"Yes!" Emma pumped her little fist. "I told Mommy you were going to be our valentine."

Alex raised his eyebrows. "Is that right?"

"Uh-huh." Features falling, she scuffed the toe of her shoe across the tiled floor. "I wish the dance was right now. Then I'd have something to do."

"I'm afraid it's been rather slow here this afternoon," Cassie explained. "It's not much fun for a little girl."

Alex scratched his chin. "Well, maybe I could help out with that a bit. I'm not on duty for another hour. Think I could convince you two to take a break and get some ice cream with me? On a sunny day like this, it's practically against the law to stay cooped up inside."

"Can we, Mom? Can we? You don't want to break the law, do you, Mom?" Emma was practically vibrating in excitement.

"How can I turn down an offer like that? Let me grab my phone in case there's an emergency, and we'll go."

Heading back to her office, she realized she was

nearly as excited as Emma. Not over the ice cream, but just from seeing Alex. Whenever she was around him her senses were heightened and her mood lifted. He made her feel good, happy with herself and her life. Just his presence, and his smiles at her daughter, were enough to have her walking on air. It was as if he was the final piece to a puzzle she'd been trying to figure out all her life. Scary, but exhilarating, too. And unlike her previous relationship, this time she would take her time and just enjoy things as they happened.

Grabbing the phone, she stuck it in her pocket and rejoined Emma and Alex. "Mollie, want me to bring you back something?"

The petite receptionist nodded at Alex. "If you run into another one of him, that would be perfect. Otherwise, a strawberry milkshake would be great."

Cassie rolled her eyes. "I'll do my best. Call me if you need me."

"Will do, boss. Have fun."

They walked outside into the kind of weather that made Florida famous. Blue skies, puffy white clouds and enough sunshine to remember that soon enough it would be summer again. The Sugar Cone was a couple of blocks down near the middle of town, an easy walk on such a nice day. She and Alex strolled hand in hand, Rex heeling beside them while Emma skipped ahead. Soon enough they were in front of the old-fashioned ice-cream parlor.

Cassie looked down at the dog; he wouldn't be allowed inside. "If you know what you want, I'll get it for you so you can stay out here with Rex."

"Two scoops of rocky road in a waffle cone. And thanks."

She nodded and followed Emma, helping her with the heavy glass door. "Do you know what you want?"

Emma pressed her face to the glass-fronted case, examining her choices. "Chocolate chip, please. In a cone."

Cassie joined her, scanning the brightly colored options. "I think I'll have mango. In a bowl, so I don't drip all over my work clothes."

"A good choice." Woody, the owner of the shop, started scooping. "Anything else?"

"Actually, yes. I need a double scoop of rocky road in a waffle cone and a strawberry milkshake, please."

"Coming right up."

Outside, they sat at one of the sidewalk tables, silent except for the occasional woof from Rex when someone he knew passed by.

"I swear, I think that dog knows more people on the island than I do," Cassie remarked after yet another person stopped to pet him.

"He's my secret weapon. I use him to get people to like me."

"Is that so?"

"Hey, it worked on you, didn't it?"

Watching him, sitting next to her daughter, eating ice cream together, she could only nod. She liked him, all right, more than she knew how to handle.

Getting into his patrol vehicle, Alex wondered how long it had been since he'd had such a simple, pleasant afternoon. A year ago, he never would have believed that watching a little girl eat ice cream would be life-changing. But watching her smile as she licked up the last bit of ice cream had made him realize that as much as he'd missed out on having a father, his father had missed out, too. Whatever demons drove him had cost him the joy of seeing his children grow up.

Alex headed away from town toward the beach road, the vastness of the horizon a counterpoint to the new view he'd stumbled upon. He'd always thought that his father had chosen adventure over the mundane, that the drab ordinariness of family life just couldn't live up to the lure of the streets. But these past few weeks with Cassie and Emma had been anything but ordinary. Being around them made everyday things better, more intense, more exciting. There was nothing boring about the way a child interacted with the world. If anything, Emma gave him a chance to see the world through new eyes, to find the fun in things that had become commonplace.

He'd worried that he couldn't be a family man because of his adrenaline-junkie ways. But the highs and lows of the past few weeks had been more intense than any he'd had on the force.

So why did men like his father and Cassie's ex leave? What made them give up what should have been the best part of their lives? The only thing he could think of was fear. The night Emma had been lost, he'd thought he might die himself. Loving a child was like having your heart out there walking around in the world, where anything could happen. From skinned knees to broken hearts, there were so many ways she could be hurt and only so much he could do to protect her. But surely the good times, the Christmas mornings and Father's Day brunches, made up for that, right?

His feelings for Cassie were just as intense. She made him want to be better than he was, to be the kind of man she deserved. She'd been through so much; just hearing about the way her ex had treated her made him sick inside. She deserved better. Emma deserved better. They deserved a man who would be there; instead, Cassie'd had to make do on her own, all while worrying that the loser might show up and demand custody one day.

Not that that seemed likely. In Alex's experience, men who abandoned their families weren't likely to show up years later, wanting to play house. Besides, wouldn't he be responsible for all that back child support? That would be a tidy sum by now, and more than enough incentive to stay lost rather than start coughing up money. Not that playing the odds was enough to calm Cassie's mind. She would have that fear hanging over her head as long as he was out there.

Alex would like nothing better than to go back in time and handle the deadbeat, man to man. He hated that the creep could still upset Cassie, and selfishly, he didn't want anything standing in the way of them building a family together.

A family. Was that really what he wanted? Pulling over, he let the car and his mind idle. Images of Cassie flashed through his head. Her gentleness with the orphaned kitten, her strength when Emma was lost, her passion and fire when they were alone together. Meeting her had changed everything, and he never wanted to go back.

He wanted to be there when she had a bad day, to find ways to make her smile or share in the laughter of a bad joke. And he wanted to be there for Emma, too. That little girl had wrapped him around her little finger the first time he saw her, and there was no pretending he didn't love her. Hell, he loved both of them.

He wanted both of them in his life, and damn it, he was going to make that happen. He'd never failed to accomplish anything he'd set his mind to and wasn't going to start now. He just needed to convince Cassie that it could work, that he could make things better for her, not worse. He needed to convince her that he was worth the risk and help her let go of the past and all the pain that had gone with it.

And he had a pretty good idea of how to start that process. He just needed to make a few phone calls to the right people.

Pulling out his personal phone, he located the number he needed and dialed.

"Ramsey, Rodriguez and Cates. How may I direct your call?"

"Ms. Cates, please. Tell her it's Alex Santiago." Now to hope that the time they'd spent working together when she was with the district attorney's office had earned him a favor. Kris Cates had a reputation for being harder than the criminals she put away, but like him, she had a soft spot for kids who'd gotten a bad rap. If he could get her to listen, she'd help.

"Alex?"

"Kris, I've got a problem, and I think you might be able to help."

Chapter Fourteen

"So are you excited about tonight?" Jillian took her lunch out of the break room microwave and stirred the spicy gumbo.

Stomach turning at the sharp smell, Cassie just nodded. Suddenly the tuna sandwich she'd packed didn't seem so appetizing.

"Are you okay? You look a bit pale."

"Just a little bit queasy. Nerves about tonight, I guess." She forced a smile and reached for a package of crackers to have with her water. Maybe the saltines would settle her stomach. Jillian had taken to stashing them around the clinic in an attempt to conquer her morning sickness.

"Oh—my—God." She stared at the package still in her hand, trembling.

Jillian's mouth dropped open as she looked at the

crackers and made the connection. "No, you don't think? I mean, could you be?"

"I didn't think so. I can't be, right? I mean, what are the odds? This is just nerves. That's all."

"Well, are you sleeping with him?"

Cassie's cool cheeks heated. "Yes, but just the one time. We decided to slow things down."

"It only takes once. You know that."

She did know, only too well. Her stomach twisted, remembering. "No way. I can't be pregnant. Alex is still getting used to the idea of Emma, and she's older. Not in diapers is what he said." Head whirling, she clutched her stomach. "Oh, God, I think I'm going to be sick."

Racing for the bathroom, she made it just in time to empty what little was in her stomach. Flashes of morning sickness with Emma came racing back, bringing on another round of retching. Behind her, the door opened a crack.

"Are you okay? Can I get you anything?"

"Um, no, I don't think so, unless you have a pregnancy test handy." Straightening up, she moved to the sink. Luckily she kept a toothbrush there for days she had garlic for lunch. Brushing her teeth and splashing some water on her face helped, but the only thing that would make her feel really better would be knowing she wasn't pregnant.

Not that she hadn't dreamed of giving Emma a sibling one day. But not like this. Not now, when she and Alex were just getting started. If he'd been cautious before, he'd be petrified now. And who could blame him?

Mollie crowded in behind Jillian. "Hey, what's going on? Why's everyone in the bathroom?"

"Cassie threw up."

So much for keeping this on the down-low. "I'm fine. I must have eaten something that didn't agree with me, that's all."

"But you didn't eat anything," Jillian protested. "You started to open those saltines I brought in, but you didn't eat any yet."

"Wait, she wanted your saltines? And she's throwing up?" Mollie turned back to Cassie, eyes wide. "Oh, my God, are you pregnant?"

"No." Having intuitive friends was really a pain sometimes.

"Maybe," Jillian countered. "You did sleep with him. You need to take a test. I have some at the inn. I can run home and get one."

"Wouldn't it be faster for me to just run to the drugstore?" Mollie asked. "If anyone asks, I'll tell them it's for a dog or something."

"You can't use them on dogs," Jillian pointed out.

"I know that, but they don't."

Cassie felt her lips twitch. Even with her world crashing down, her friends could still make her smile. "Fine. Mollie, take some cash from my purse and go get a test. And maybe some ginger ale for my stomach. All this crazy talk about pregnancy is making it worse. Then once you both see that it's negative, we can move on with our day."

Two lines. That couldn't be right. Maybe they'd changed the tests since she'd taken that one five years ago. With shaking hands, she grabbed the box back out of the trash and read the instructions again. And again.

Deflating like a balloon, she slid down the wall, landing in a pile on the floor. She was pregnant. And just like before, she was going to have to figure things out on her own. At least this time she knew what to expect. She wouldn't be scared by Braxton Hicks or looking up the symptoms of colic online at 3:00 a.m. She knew how to take care of a baby. What she didn't know was how to tell Alex.

She needed to do it now before he started getting any more pie-in-the-sky ideas about a relationship with her. She grimaced. If she'd wanted a surefire way to scare him off, she'd found it. Breaking the news on a second date should pretty much guarantee there wouldn't be a third, not after he had made such a big deal about wanting to slow things down. Having a baby together was pretty much the opposite of that.

But before telling him, she had to face her friends. From her spot on the floor, she called them. "You can come in."

Both women squeezed into the tiny room. Jillian went to Cassie, but Mollie dove for the test on the sink. Holding it up, she squinted, then passed it to Jillian. "You're pregnant. You must know how to read these things."

Jillian took one look and started crying. "Oh, my goodness, you're pregnant—we're going to be pregnant together!" Taking the Kleenex a bewildered Mollie handed her, she blew her nose. "I'm sorry, honey. I know you're more upset than excited. But really, it's going to be wonderful. Just think, our babies will grow up together."

Okay, so maybe she wasn't alone this time. She'd have her friends; that meant something. And it would be fun to be pregnant together; she'd never had a mom friend before. Sniffling, she took the tissues from Jillian. "Look what you did. Now I'm crying."

Mollie looked from one crying woman to the other. "Hell, if this is contagious, I'm getting out of here."

Laughing through her tears, Cassie shook her head. "Trust me. That's not how it happens." Sobering, she stood up, pulling Jillian with her. "Seriously, though, what am I going to do?"

"For starters," Mollie said, "we're all going to get out of this bathroom. This is getting weird. Then, Jillian's going to put the Closed sign up—you planned on closing early anyway because of the dance—and cancel whatever appointments are left. Then we can all go have some ice cream or a pedicure or whatever it is girls are supposed to do when bonding. We'll figure out everything else together."

Jillian nodded, tears forming again. "She's right. No matter what happens with Alex, you and that baby are going to be loved to pieces."

Looking from one woman to the other, Cassie had to smile. Her luck with men might be lousy, but she sure knew how to pick her friends.

Alex nailed the last board in the makeshift bandstand into place. In a few hours, this place would be transformed, and it felt good to know he'd played a part. Smiling, he pictured himself dancing with Cassie in front of the bandstand later tonight. He couldn't wait to get his hands on her, even if it was in the middle of a crowded room.

"What're you grinning about?" Nic wiped the sweat off his face with the bottom of his T-shirt. "We've been working like dogs for hours, and you're grinning like a fool."

"No. I'm not. I'm just picturing what it's all going to look like when it's done."

Nic smiled knowingly. "You're picturing Cassie all dressed up in something slinky. That's what you're thinking about."

"Hey, watch it."

Nic held his hands up. "No harm meant. Seems like you're pretty serious about her, huh?"

Alex dusted his hands on his jeans, then met the other man's gaze. "I think so, yeah. I don't know that she's ready for anything serious, but I'm hoping I can convince her."

"And you're okay with her having a kid? Not every guy wants to take on a family all at once like that."

"I'm more than okay with it. I thought I wouldn't be. My dad wasn't exactly father of the year, and I just didn't want to even get into the whole family thing. But Emma's great. Kids are great. Heck, I don't have to convince you. You're having one of your own soon."

Nic took a swig from a bottle of water, swallowing hard. "Yeah, it's kind of terrifying, but in a good way, you know? I mean, there are so many ways to screw up, but still, I can't wait to have a son to teach things to, do things with, you know?"

"Wait, it's a boy? You found out already?"

Nic grimaced. "Uh, yeah. But can you pretend you didn't hear that? Jillian wants to wait a bit before we tell people, so she can do a big announcement or something. She'll kill me if she finds out I told you."

"Hey, no problem, man. I don't want to get you in any trouble. In fact, I'd appreciate it if you didn't say anything about my intentions with Cassie. I don't want to scare her off by moving too fast."

"Intentions? What exactly are you thinking here? Marriage?"

"I know it sounds crazy, but yeah, eventually. I think it will take some time to get her to trust me, but I'm in this for the long haul." Just saying it made him feel as if he'd won the lottery—how much better would the real thing be?

"Congrats, man." Nic slapped him on the back and handed him an unopened bottle of water. "Here's to new beginnings."

"I'll drink to that."

Taking a deep drink, he realized Nic was becoming a real friend. He'd made a few buddies in the department since moving here, but it was a different kind of friendship. He relied on them to watch his back, but he couldn't see talking to them about his relationship problems or anything like that. That was likely his own fault; after what had happened in Miami, he'd kept to himself, afraid to let his guard down. Maybe it was time to work on that, too. After all, he'd told himself Paradise was going to be a fresh start, the place where he put down some roots. Cassie was part of that, but if he was going to build a life here, he'd need to put in the effort and meet people halfway.

"You going to stand there looking dreamy-eyed all day or get some work done? We've still got to hang the lights and set up the tables."

"Yeah, I'm going to help, but let's hurry, okay? I want to swing by the florist before I pick up Cassie and Emma." He was going to make sure tonight was a night they'd never forget.

Chapter Fifteen

Cassie nervously twisted her hair around a finger, checking her image in the mirror. Did she look pregnant? Would everyone be able to tell? Would Alex be able to tell?

"You look fine." Mollie took her hand and led her away from the mirror. "Better than fine. You look amazing. Alex is going to flip when he sees you. If he's not in love with you already, he will be when he sees you in that dress."

"I don't think a dress is going to do any such thing." Although she did look good in it. The red material clung to her curves, draping nearly to the floor. The neckline showed just a hint of cleavage, but the back was cut away nearly to her waist, and a slit exposed her thigh every time she took a step. If seduction was a dress, it would be this dress. Too bad it would go to waste tonight. Seduction was what had gotten her into this predicament.

"Where's Emma? She's usually in here underfoot when I'm getting dressed."

"She's making up another batch of Valentine's Day cards in the kitchen. Don't worry. I told her, no glue, glitter or paint."

"Thank you." It had taken forever to get Emma to choose a dress; if she ruined it, they would never get her in another one.

"So, are you going to tell her about the new baby?"

Cassie checked to be sure the bedroom door was still closed. "Not yet. I'll have to eventually, especially if the morning sickness keeps up. But I want to talk to Alex first. I need to figure out where things stand before she starts asking a zillion questions."

"So you're definitely going to keep it?"

"Absolutely." There was no doubt in her mind about that. She'd had her crying fit this afternoon, but her maternal instincts were already kicking in. "It's going to be hard, but I've done the single mom thing before, and I can do it again. Besides, this time I have you guys to help."

"You know, it might not be like that, not this time. Alex isn't Tony. He's not going to take off. He's too responsible for that."

"Maybe. It would be nice if he was part of this baby's life. But I'm not going to count on it." She'd been burned before. And selfishly she dreaded the idea of working out a visitation schedule. She'd heard horror stories about ugly custody battles and didn't want to fight over a baby as if it was a prized toy instead of a family member. Of course, given Alex's feelings on children, it might not come to that.

Mollie tugged at the hemline of her dress. "Well, I'll be there for moral support if you need it. Although I'm not sure how long I'm going to last. Why couldn't we have had a casual fundraiser, like a fish fry or something? I could wear shorts to a fish fry."

"You look gorgeous. And you're going to be too busy fighting off eligible men to even think about what you're wearing."

Mollie rolled her eyes. "I doubt it. Besides, I'm going to be hanging out with Emma so you and Alex can have your talk. Unless you aren't going to tell him tonight? You could always wait a bit before you say anything."

"No, I have to tell him before he starts getting any more ideas about us. No use putting off the inevitable. Besides, once Emma knows, everyone in town will know. She can't keep a secret for more than a millisecond."

"I see your point."

A knock at the front door ended the conversation and sent Cassie's pulse skyrocketing.

"Want me to get it?"

Cassie nodded. "Please." Taking a few deep breaths, she reminded herself that everything would be okay. Alex might be angry, but she could handle that. She just needed to get through the night; then she'd worry about everything else.

Forcing herself into the living room, her heart jumped at the sight of him. He always looked good, but wow, could he rock a tux. He would have fit right in on a red carpet somewhere in Hollywood. For a moment, she let herself pretend that nothing had changed, that they were just two people having a romantic evening. Maybe she could wait just a little longer before she ruined it all.

But the longer she held on, the harder it would be to let him go. Better to do it and get it over with. But not here—she'd wait until they'd finished with their duties at the dance. The kids were counting on everyone to make the dance a success, and her personal problems shouldn't stand in the way of that.

Alex turned and saw her standing in the hallway. "You look amazing. I'm going to be the envy of the island tonight with you on my arm."

"And me," Emma added, twirling to show off her dress.

Kneeling, Alex slipped a tiny corsage over her wrist. "Of course. In fact, I think you'll be the prettiest one there."

Enchanted, Emma examined the flowers while Alex crossed over to Cassie. "I got one for you, too. Here, let me." She held still while he pinned a tasteful white orchid spray to her dress. Could he feel how hard her heart was beating? The scent of his cologne teased her, making her want to forget everything and just bury her head against his chest.

"Are you okay?" he asked, a concerned frown on his face. "You seem awfully quiet."

"She's just worried about getting there on time, that's all," Mollie interjected. "In fact, we really should be going. Mrs. Rosenberg will have a fit if we're late."

"She's right." Cassie nodded, grateful for her friend's quick thinking. "Let's hit the road." The sooner they left, the sooner the whole night would be over, and she could start finding a way forward.

* * *

Alex carefully buckled Emma's car seat into the backseat of his SUV, then helped the little girl climb in.

Emma sat up straight as he adjusted the straps, then surprised him with a kiss on the cheek. "Thank you for being my valentine."

Swallowing past the lump in his throat, he smiled. "No, thank you." He'd always considered himself a tough, masculine kind of man, but he was no match for a four-year-old in a party dress. Cassie had already let herself into the car and was ready to go, so he climbed in and started the engine. Mollie was going to follow in her own car. "So, which one of you do I get to dance with first?"

"Me! Pick me," Emma called from the back.

"All right, you got it. But you have to let me dance with your mommy, too."

"I know that. She's your valentine, too, so you have to dance with her."

Cassie just nodded while looking out the window. She'd been awfully quiet since he picked her up. Was she worried about the event? Or had he done something wrong?

"Hey, everything okay?" he asked in a low voice, mindful of Emma in the back.

"Hmm? Oh, sure, everything's fine. I just have a lot on my mind."

"Mommy didn't feel good earlier. She had a tummy ache. I heard Mollie say so."

So much for keeping the conversation private. "Are you sick? You don't have to go if you aren't feeling well. I can explain to everyone."

"No, I'm fine. Just a minor case of nerves, or maybe

something I ate. I'm fine now. Besides, Emma would be heartbroken."

"I could still take Emma—"

"I said I'm fine."

Taken aback by her sharp tone, he let it drop. Maybe she didn't trust him to take Emma by himself, which kind of stung. Or maybe she really was fine, although her color seemed a bit off. Either way, he was going to keep a close eye on her tonight. If she started feeling bad, he'd insist on taking her home.

She was quiet the rest of the way to the Sandpiper, but Emma kept up a constant chatter to fill the gap. It seemed she was most looking forward to the cupcakes and seeing Mrs. Rosenberg, whom for some reason she adored. He was half in awe, half terrified of the woman himself.

Soon enough he was pulling into the packed parking lot. Not spotting any open spaces, he idled for a minute. "Why don't you ladies get out here, and I'll go find a spot on the street."

Once his passengers were safely on their way, he circled back out and found a parking spot a block away. It seemed most of the town had come out early to be sure everything was ready. Luckily the kids were coming by bus, so they wouldn't have to walk too far. Hiking back, he wondered if expanding the parking lot was in Nic's renovation plans.

Up at the main entrance, the streamers he'd helped hang were blowing gently in the wind, illuminated by twinkling white lights. Mrs. Rosenberg stood sentry at the front door, decked out in a fluorescent-pink sequined dress and a corsage the size of a dinner plate. Waving her clipboard, she flagged him down. "I need you to help fill the coolers with ice. And then after that, the ladies in the kitchen will need some help carrying the food trays out."

"Yes, ma'am." He hoped she didn't keep him running all night; he had a few dances to claim.

As if reading his mind, she winked at him. "And then go find Cassie and her girl. Enjoy yourself. You've earned it."

Letting out a breath, he thanked her and made a beeline for the kitchen before she thought of any other projects for him to do. On his way he passed Jillian, looking radiant and starting to show. "You look beautiful. Nic's a lucky man."

She blushed and put a hand on her belly. "Thank you. I'm afraid I feel a bit oversize at the moment. My scrubs at work are a lot more forgiving than evening wear."

"Like I said, beautiful." And he meant it. He thought of how Cassie must have looked carrying Emma and was sorry he'd missed it. Maybe someday they'd have a child of their own. That thought would have terrified him a few months ago. Now it just seemed the natural way of things. They'd date, get to know each other better, and down the road, who knew? The future was wide-open.

He'd moved ten bags of ice and carried out more baked goods than he'd seen in a lifetime before he was able to look for Cassie. He checked the lobby, which seemed to be the gathering spot for the island's senior set, then moved to the back porch. Parents and children sat eating cake at tables covered in pink-and-white tablecloths. Winding his way through them, he was stopped every few feet by people he'd met while volunteering or out on the job. It struck him that he'd made more friends in his short time in Paradise than he had in a lifetime in Miami. Not because the people in Paradise were so much different, but because he was different. He'd grown up protecting himself from being let down, but what he'd really done was isolate himself. For whatever reason, being forced to start over had helped him get past that.

"Deputy Alex, come see!"

Emma was at a smaller, child-size table set up on the part of the patio that wrapped around the side of the building. Covering the table were markers, paper and various odds and ends. Several other children were huddled around the table with her, studiously working on what must be some kind of Valentine's Day craft. "What did you make?"

"It's a Valentine's Day spider! See, it's red and has candy stuck in its web instead of flies."

Trying not to laugh, he picked up the paper. "Wow, that's really creative."

"Thank you. Now can we dance? I've been waiting forever."

"Absolutely. I promised, didn't I? And I always keep my promises."

Cassie watched Alex and Emma walk onto the makeshift dance floor and felt another piece of her heart break. Emma looked so happy, gazing up at Alex as if he was the father she'd never had. How would she take it when she found out there was going to be a baby that really was Alex's? Would she be jealous if he turned his attention from her to the baby? Or worse, if Alex wasn't willing or able to be there for this child, would it shatter the dreams Emma had built up about what a father was?

Cassie would have given anything to fix this for her little girl, but it was out of her hands. Once Alex knew, it was up to him. And he'd been perfectly honest with her about his issues around fatherhood. He'd asked to take things slow, and she was throwing them both into the fast lane.

Jillian stepped up beside her and followed her gaze. "You know, you might be wrong about him. That doesn't look like a man who is afraid of children. In fact, he looks pretty smitten with your little girl."

"I'm sure he likes Emma, but—"

"Cassie, Alex isn't Tony. You need to stop expecting him to act like Tony. Give him a chance. Go talk to him." She gave Cassie a little push. "And if you need me, I'll be over at the refreshment table, loading up on key lime pie. Just look for the lady eating for two. Now stop standing here staring and go get your man."

Not having any better ideas, Cassie started down the stairs toward Alex and Emma. Spotting her, Alex waved. "Honey, I think it's your mommy's turn for a dance. Why don't you go find some of those cupcakes you were talking about?"

Energized at the thought of the treats, she darted off in a blur of pink lace.

Alex shook his head. "Where does she get her energy?"

"Well, I think it helps that she still gets an afternoon nap."

He chuckled. "I'll have to try that sometime. How about you? Are you feeling any better?"

She nodded, not wanting to open that can of worms

just yet. "Didn't you promise me a dance?" One dance couldn't hurt, right? And he looked so good in his tuxedo, she just couldn't resist. She'd be strong later; right now she just wanted to lean into him and let the music carry her away. Taking his hand, she let him lead her onto the floor and pull her close enough to melt against him.

"Have I told you how beautiful you look in that dress?"

She shook her head, not trusting her voice.

"Well, you do. You're absolutely stunning. Of course, you always are."

In a few months, he might not think so. Soon she'd be too big around for anyone to consider her stunning. Choking back her sob, she forced herself to try to enjoy the moment.

"I've been thinking." Alex's deep voice resonated through her body. "I know I said I want to take things slowly, but I think you should know how I'm feeling. The truth is, I'm crazy about you."

Looking up, she kept her voice in check. "And what about kids? You said you weren't sure you'd ever be ready for them."

"I know, but the more I'm around Emma, the more I'm crazy about her, too. And it's not like you're talking about a houseful of kids. It's just Emma, and she's wonderful, like her mother."

Wonderful. Except in about nine months, it wouldn't be just Emma anymore. Screwing up her courage, she stopped dancing. "Listen, Alex, we need to talk."

"I thought that's what we were doing." Confusion filled his eyes.

"Oh, there you are, Alex." Mrs. Rosenberg appeared at the edge of the dance floor. "I'm afraid I must pull you away for just a moment. We need someone strong enough to move some crates in the kitchen, and I can't find anyone else."

Cassie stepped back, dropping her arms from his shoulders. "Go. I should go check on Emma, anyway."

Hesitantly he walked away, leaving her alone on the dance floor.

"Hey, there's my girl. Did you save a dance for your old man?" Her father smiled, and she felt tears prick her eyes.

"Sure, Dad." Placing her hand in his, she let him lead her slowly around the floor. He was still a bit stiff, but he did remarkably well, given that he'd stopped using the cane only a few days ago. Soon he'd be back at the office, a godsend, considering the circumstances. Her parents had given her so much support when she'd had Emma, and they would again. That was one thing to be grateful for.

"What's going on, sweetie? Are you crying?" He offered her a freshly starched handkerchief from his suit pocket.

Hastily wiping the tears away, she smiled. "I was just thinking how lucky I am to have you and Mom." It was the truth; she did have the best parents. She just hated to disappoint them again.

"Well, I'm not sure what brought that on, but thank you. We're pretty proud of you, too. But speaking of your mother, I'd better go rest this leg before she catches me down here and makes a scene."

Giving him a quick squeeze, she smiled and watched him limp up the stairs to the patio, where, sure enough, her mother was watching, concern on her face. Her parents had that rare kind of love usually found only in romance novels and love songs. She'd always assumed she'd have that kind of relationship one day, but so far she hadn't even managed a long-term boyfriend, let alone a successful marriage.

Heading for the back of the inn, she tried to smile and be polite to everyone, while inside all she wanted was to go home and curl up in her bed until morning. But first she needed to tell Alex about the pregnancy. She'd never be able to sleep otherwise. She found him in the kitchen, holding Emma up to the sink so she could wash her hands. Such a simple thing and a reminder of what might have been.

"Hi, Mommy. I ate two cupcakes!"

"That she did, although how much she ate versus how much was on her hands, I'm not sure. I figured we'd better get her cleaned up before she got chocolate all over her pretty dress." He set Emma down and handed her a paper towel.

"Thanks. I appreciate it."

"Can I go play with the other kids now? Miss Jillian said there were going to be games on the side porch."

"Sure. I'll come watch in a little bit."

Once Emma was out of earshot, she turned back to Alex, her hands clenched in front of her.

"We need to talk."

Chapter Sixteen

Alex carefully finished drying his hands, taking the time to fold the dishtowel he'd used and hang it back up on its hook. He was in no hurry to hear what Cassie was about to say; the look on her face made it clear this wasn't good news. Besides, he'd dated enough women to know that "we need to talk" was relationship speak for "I want to break up." He should have realized something was off when she was so quiet earlier. But he'd been so caught up in how he was feeling, he hadn't stopped to think if she was in the same place.

No, he'd just come out and told her that he was crazy about her, basically said he loved her, and then left her standing there while he played pack mule for Mrs. Rosenberg. Not exactly the most romantic way to handle things. He must have scared her, read the signals wrong.

"If this is about what I said earlier, if I came on too strong—"

"No, it's not that." She looked over her shoulder nervously. "I'd rather talk somewhere more private, if that's okay."

This was definitely not good. But he needed to hear what she had to say before he could come up with an argument, so he just shrugged. "Sure. Nic and Jillian are outside supervising the games. We could use their office."

She didn't say anything, just went down the short hallway that led to the private suite of rooms separate from the public side of the inn. A small, comfortably-furnished office doubled as a sitting room and had a thick oak door that Cassie closed behind them. "You might want to sit down."

"I'm fine, thanks." He'd stand on his own two feet and handle this like a man.

"Well, when Emma said I wasn't feeling well, that was partly right."

"Wait, are you sick? Is it something serious?" Words like *cancer* and *multiple sclerosis* cluttered his head.

She managed a sad smile. "No, I'm not sick, not really. But there is something serious going on." She twisted her hands, her knuckles turning white. "You remember our night together after Emma was lost?"

"Of course I do. It was the most amazing night of my life." What on earth did this have to do with her feeling sick? Unless… But she'd said the timing wasn't right. That couldn't be it. "You're not saying you're pregnant, are you?"

"I'm sorry." Her voice cracked, but she kept her head up and her shoulders straight. There was fear in her eyes, but strength as well. "I just found out today. I didn't know how to tell you, or if I should tell you—"

"If you should tell me?" Voice rising, he tried to keep his temper in check. "How could you even consider not telling me?" Another thought intruded. "Are you even sure? You said you didn't think it was the right time."

"Do you think I'd be having this conversation with you if I wasn't sure? Do you want to see the test with the two lines?" Her eyes narrowed. "Or are you questioning if it's yours?"

Was he? No, not really. They'd never said they were exclusive, but he didn't think she was the type to be dating multiple men. Which meant, if she was right, all his doubts about becoming a father didn't matter. He was going to be one, ready or not.

Sweat pooled along his back as the full impact of what she was saying hit him. He opened his mouth, then closed it again, not wanting to say the wrong thing. Finally, realizing he hadn't answered her question, he shook his head. "No, I believe you. I just don't know what I'm supposed to say. I don't know what to do."

Silent tears marked her face. "Well, the good news is that you don't have to do a damned thing. I've done this on my own before, and I'll do it again."

"Cassie, no, I didn't mean that. Of course I'm willing to do whatever I need to—"

She threw her hands up, determination written on her face. "No, stop right there. I don't want my baby to have a father who's there just because he thinks he's supposed to be. You made it very clear how you felt about fatherhood and having kids. I'm not asking you for anything. I just thought you should know before anything more happened between us. Now, if you'll excuse me, I'm feeling tired and I'd like to go home."

He ran a hand through his hair, too confused to argue. "Fine, I'll go get the car."

"Don't. I think it's better if I have Mollie drive Emma and me home." She was openly crying now. He wanted to go to her, to comfort her, but she would surely push him away. So he just stood there, helpless, while the woman he loved walked out the door.

Half blinded by tears and emotion, Cassie nearly ran Jillian over on her way down the hall. "Oh, my God, I'm sorry, Jillian. Are you okay?"

"I'm fine." She reached out and steadied herself against Cassie, assessing her friend. "More to the point, are you okay?"

Cassie sniffed and rubbed at her eyes. "Not really, but I will be. I just need to get home and have some space to figure things out."

Jillian's eyes filled with sympathy. "So you told him?"

"I did. And he was shocked, and confused, and doesn't know what he wants to do. Which is a luxury he gets to have, being a man. I, however, know what I need to do. I need to get my child and get home, and then start rearranging my entire life to accommodate a baby that *is* coming, like it or not."

Jillian's jaw dropped open. "He didn't say you shouldn't keep the baby?"

"No, nothing like that." Thank goodness. That might have really sent her over the edge. "He just really didn't have much to say at all."

"Well, he probably needs some time to process everything. Even Nic was a bit overwhelmed when I broke the news to him."

"The difference is, Nic wanted a baby. You two were actively trying, so you knew he would come around. Alex and I were definitely not trying. He once said fatherhood wasn't even on his radar. So I don't think I'll hold my breath."

"I don't know if he's lying to you or to himself, but something isn't right here. I've seen him with Emma. He adores her. And don't forget, he was the first one to sign up for the new mentor program. And he's spent hours of his personal time helping to make this dance a success so that those kids get what they need. He even came and helped make those silly heart decorations, remember? Does that sound like a guy who shirks commitment? I'm telling you, you need to give him a chance. Don't you remember how upset you were when you found out today? And you had Mollie and me there with you to support you. So maybe just give him some time, okay?"

That all sounded logical, but in her experience men seldom were logical in this kind of situation. Still, she'd at least think about what Jillian had said. "Fine, he can have time. Nine months, in fact. But for now, please, I just want to go home and go to bed."

"Why don't you go wash your face and freshen up a bit? I'll find Emma and Mollie and meet you out front in a few minutes."

"Thanks."

In the bathroom, she scrubbed off her ruined mascara and tried to finger comb her hair into some semblance of normalcy. No need to scare Emma—not that her rambunctious daughter was likely to notice after all the excitement. Thankfully it was a clear shot to the front door from here, so she wasn't likely to run into many guests. Taking a deep breath, she checked that the coast was clear and made it outside without seeing anyone. Emma and Mollie were already waiting on the stairs, looking through the party favors in Emma's goody bag.

"Hi, guys, ready to go?"

"Do we have to go already?" Emma protested with a yawn.

"Yes, sleepyhead. It's way past your bedtime, and mine, too."

"Then why isn't Deputy Alex taking us home? He brought us here. Shouldn't he drive us back?"

"He wanted to, but he has to stay and help clean up," Mollie said brightly. "That's why I'm taking you home. I don't like to clean up."

"Me, either." Emma let herself be buckled in without any more protests or questions and a few minutes later was softly snoring.

"Thank you for the ride, and everything."

"Hey, that's what friends are for. That, and babysitting. All I ask is first dibs on baby snuggles."

A baby. She was going to have a baby. She'd been so busy freaking out about it she hadn't let herself think about the good parts. First smiles and the smell of baby powder, things she'd treasured with Emma and was going to get to do all over again. Her heart might be broken, but a baby was a pretty amazing thing. She needed to remember that and focus on the good things to come.

At the house, she gave Mollie a hard hug. "Keep reminding me about the baby snuggles, okay?"

"Anytime. Now go to bed and get some sleep. You look like hell."

Mollie's smile tempered her words, and anyway, she was right. Exhaustion didn't begin to describe the level of tired Cassie was at right now. Lifting Emma out of the seat, she managed to carry the sleeping girl inside without waking her. Helping her use the potty and change her into a nightgown was a little trickier, but soon she was tucked into bed, looking too sweet to be real. On impulse, Cassie bent down and gave her an extra kiss, saying a silent prayer that no matter what happened, they'd all come out of this stronger and happier. Because no matter how her heart hurt, her children were counting on her.

Alex stacked the last of the folding chairs, leaving the Sandpiper's wide, whitewashed porch looking oddly deserted after the chaos of the evening. Since Cassie's big announcement, he'd been on autopilot, mindlessly moving from task to task. Stacking chairs, taking down decorations, sweeping floors; those were things he knew how to do. How to handle the situation with Cassie? He didn't have a clue. Obviously, considering she'd left in tears.

He still didn't know what to think, let alone what to do. So he grabbed the chairs and carried them to the storage building. As long as there was still work to be done, he could avoid everything else. Maybe that would give his shell-shocked brain time to start working again.

He was on his way back when Nic stepped out from the darkness, walking Murphy on a long leash. "I'm surprised you're still here. Jillian told me what happened with Cassie."

"What happened is, I let my hormones override my common sense. It's not like I'm a dumb teenager. I know how to use protection. I let her down, and now she's furious with me."

Nic stared at him. "That's what you got from your talk with her? That she's mad at you for getting her pregnant?"

"Well, yeah. Hell, I'm mad at myself. But I'm not the one who has to go through the whole labor and delivery thing."

Nic shook his head. "You, my friend, are an idiot. She's not angry—she's terrified."

"She sure seemed angry."

"Well, maybe she was looking for some support from you. Some kind of solidarity, given the situation."

He thought back. He hadn't really offered any support; he'd been too busy asking questions. Questions that, in retrospect, made him sound like a jerk. "Right. Man, I messed up. She must hate me. First, the condom broke. Then, when she tells me she's pregnant, all I can do is ask stupid questions."

Nic chuckled and slapped him on the back. "I think that's a pretty normal male reaction. But you've got to move past that. She's going to need you."

Cassie was so strong, it was hard to imagine her needing anyone, but Nic was right. She was carrying Alex's child, and that meant she was going to have to accept his involvement in her life, no matter how upset she was with him. She was carrying his child, and that gave him rights.

His child. *Dios mío*, he was going to be a father. Knees buckling, he leaned against a tree and tried to breathe normally. He'd sort of come to grips with the idea of someday, maybe, being a stepfather to Emma. But that was far in the future; this was happening now.

Or sometime in the next nine months, anyway. Besides, Emma was older. Babies were different; they had floppy heads and you could break them if you held them wrong. And they couldn't tell you what they needed—they just cried. How on earth was he supposed to know how to take care of a baby?

"It's scary stuff, huh?" Nic asked, grinning.

How could he just stand there with that stupid look on his face? "Scary? It's terrifying. I'm not qualified for this."

"None of us are, my friend. But you'll learn. Look at it like a new assignment. You'll study up, maybe do some on-the-job training, and whatever you don't learn ahead of time, you'll figure out as you go. At least Cassie's done this before. Jillian and I are both rookies. Now, that's frightening."

Despite himself, Alex smiled. He did have a veteran partner—if she was still interested in being his partner. That he might have permanently ruined his chances with Cassie was more frightening than the idea of becoming a father. Which meant he needed to fix things. The baby, he'd figure that out. But letting Cassie go was unthinkable.

Pushing himself up from the tree, he broke into a jog toward his car.

"Hey, what are you going to do?"

"Whatever it takes."

Chapter Seventeen

The coffee and stress of the past several hours were wearing a hole in his stomach, but Alex wasn't ready to quit yet. Night shifts were nothing new, and although he preferred footwork to computer searches, he wasn't going to complain. He'd spent the night reaching out to contacts down south, working his way along a web of information. Thankfully, many of them kept the same odd hours he did and worked quickly and discreetly. A few minutes ago, he'd found what he thought was his target, and now all he could do was wait. If his information was right he'd know soon.

Too keyed up to sleep, he checked a few sports stats and then, feeling foolish, found himself searching for baby-care websites. Close to an hour later, he had a half-page of notes in front of him and more questions than when he started. It seemed he'd underestimated the number of ways one could injure or maim a baby. Everything from what position they slept in to when they had their first bite of food seemed to be imbued with the potential for danger. And that was just in the first year of life. What the websites didn't say was that there would be bullies and book reports and bad dates, and no way to protect them from it all. How could he ever have thought parenting would be boring?

And before that even started, there was the pregnancy to get through, and after that the birth itself. He hadn't been brave enough to watch any of the birth videos he'd come across, but he'd read enough to freak himself out. Of course, Cassie was the one dealing with that, but he didn't intend for her to face it alone.

He couldn't carry the baby for those nine months, but he could try to make Cassie's life easier, handle what could be handled. Which was why he'd been on his laptop all night when he should have been sleeping. If he could track down Cassie's ex, find out where he was, if he was coming back and what his intentions toward Emma were, maybe he could ease some of the burden she'd carried for the past five years.

Of course, there was the chance he would stir something up and make more trouble. That's why he hadn't followed up yet on the information his lawyer friend had sent over. He hadn't wanted to risk making things worse. But the stakes were different now. If he was ever going to have a chance at a real family with Cassie, he needed to know where he stood, and so did she. Always looking over her shoulder was keeping her from looking ahead, and they'd never be able to plan a future together that way. And if he was going to be in Emma's life, he needed to know everything he could about her, and that meant knowing about the man who had fathered her.

Getting up to refill his coffee mug, he nearly tripped over Rex. The big dog had sensed something was up and had been at his side all night. "You need to go out?" Rex thumped his tail and rose, stretching leisurely the way only animals and small children seem to do. He let the dog out and then filled his mug with the overheated dregs from the pot. If he hadn't heard anything by the time he finished this cup, he'd try to get some sleep.

As if on cue, his email alert chimed. Straddling his chair, he clicked on the newest message and quickly scanned the text. Got him! It seemed Tony Williams was now a first mate aboard a sport-fishing boat in the Bahamas. Alex's contact over there said the boat was operating out of Nassau, less than two hours away by plane. He could shower, drop Rex off, catch a flight out of Orlando and be there by lunchtime. And after that? It was anyone's guess.

Cassie woke at dawn to a kitten purring in her ear. Pushing the little gray monster away did no good; the kitten was relentless when it came to food. Her eyes shut, she tried to ignore the cat climbing onto her chest, his sharp nails pricking her skin as he kneaded her with his front paws. She didn't want to wake up. As long as she was asleep, she didn't have to think about Alex, or the baby, or the million other things demanding immediate attention. At least the clinic was closed. She'd anticipated spending her Saturday recuperating after a late night at the dance. That she'd be dealing with morning sickness and a broken heart had never occurred to her.

Sensing she was awake, Trouble began meowing.

Not a quiet, demure mew, but a full-blown meow that
made it sound as if he was in danger of actually starving
to death. Giving up, she lifted him off her and sat up,
petting the cat to keep him quiet. She could really use
a few minutes of quiet before Emma woke up. "Keep
the volume down, and I'll feed you, okay?"

She pulled on her robe and shuffled into the kitchen,
the kitten darting between her legs and generally being
a nuisance. He was really lucky he was cute. Putting
the kettle to boil, she opened a small can of cat food
and dumped it into a saucer on the floor. Delighted,
the roly-poly critter pounced, nearly upsetting the dish.
Grinning at his antics despite herself, she leaned on the
counter and waited for the water to boil.

Once she'd made her tea, she eased open the sliding
door and settled into her favorite chair on the patio. The
hot mug warmed her hands, and she tucked her feet up
under her robe against the early morning chill. Dew
clung to the leaves of her orchids, and in the distance,
a woodpecker was drilling for his breakfast. This was
her happy place, her personal oasis from the bustle of
everyday life. Right now she had half a dozen different
plants in bloom, and on the breeze there was the first
hint of the season's orange blossoms.

Alex had never been out here, never seen this little
corner of her world. There were a million little things
about each other they didn't know. But when she was
with him, that hadn't mattered. They'd shared the important things, the things that made them who they
were. She knew about his father and his fears for his
own future. And he knew about Tony, and the accident,
and the pressure she was under. She'd thought that had
been enough.

"Mommy, where are you?"

"I'm on the patio, sweetie."

Emma's face peeked around the door, her eyes still glassy from sleep. "It's cold out there."

"Then I guess I'd better come in, hadn't I?" Getting up, she took a last look at her flowers, then scooped Emma into her arms and carried her to the kitchen. Setting her on a stool, she rinsed her mug in the sink. "So, what should we do for breakfast today?"

"We should have pancakes and bacon. I love bacon."

Cassie's stomach flip-flopped. Bacon didn't sound so good to her right now. Actually, cooking suddenly sounded like more trouble than it was worth. "What if we go out for breakfast instead? We could pick up some muffins and then take them over to the Sandpiper and have a picnic in the yard. How does that sound?"

Emma pumped her little fist. "Yes! Muffins and juice?"

She ruffled the little girl's strawberry-blond curls, so like her own. Would this new baby look like her or like Alex? "Yes, juice, too." In fact, juice and plain toast sounded like the perfect breakfast to settle her queasy stomach. "We'll go as soon as you're dressed and ready."

The lure of blueberry muffins had Emma dressed in record time. Cassie didn't take much longer, not bothering to do more than walk through a quick shower and throw on jeans and a T-shirt. She really needed to spend the day doing laundry and catching up on housework, but she was as eager to get out of the house as Emma. Some fresh air and time with Jillian would help clear the fog from her head. Then she could focus and start working on a plan.

Emma kept up a one-sided conversation about last night's festivities as they drove to and from the bakery, stopping only when they pulled into the gravel lot of the Sandpiper. "Can we have our picnic now, right away?"

Cassie freed Emma from her seat and grabbed the bakery box full of muffins. "Let's go up and say hello to Miss Jillian and Mr. Nic and see if they want some muffins. Then you and Murphy can have a picnic together."

Not bothering to reply, Emma tore off toward the front door. Following more slowly, Cassie was just turning off the path when not one, but two dogs came running up. "Hey, Rex, what are you doing here?" Stalling, she stopped and petted both dogs. She wasn't ready to face Alex yet. She was barely able to face herself. But Emma was expecting a picnic, which meant there was no going back.

Squaring her shoulders, she followed the path up to the inn, where Emma was waiting on the stairs for her. "Did you see, Mom? Rex is here, so he can come to the picnic with Murphy."

"So it seems." Unless she was lucky and Alex was just leaving. Why would he be here, anyway, and so early in the morning? Pounding up the stairs to the front door, she held the door for Emma and her four-legged buddies. Not finding anyone at the front desk, she headed back to the kitchen, where Jillian was mixing up some kind of batter at the counter.

"Are you making pancakes?" Emma stood on her toes, trying to see into the bowl.

"I sure am. With blueberries in them. Do you want some?"

"Yes, please." Emma nodded, eyes wide. "I wanted

pancakes, but Mommy took us to get muffins instead. Now I can have muffins and pancakes on my picnic."

Familiar with Emma's little adventures Jillian didn't bat an eye. "Then I'll make sure to pack some up for you. Just don't let Murphy eat them."

"Or Rex," Emma added.

Jillian stirred harder, not looking up from the bowl. "Right, or Rex. Listen, Emma, why don't you take a muffin out to the yard, and then I'll bring you some pancakes when they're ready?"

"Okay." Emma carefully extracted an oversize muffin from the bakery box, then headed out the open back door, Rex and Murphy at her side.

"So, why is Rex here, Jillian? And where's Alex?"

Jillian wiped her hands, coming over to sit next to Cassie at the old oak table that dominated the kitchen. "We're dog sitting. But listen, it's not what you think."

What? Where the heck was Alex that he couldn't take Rex with him? They went everywhere together. "What do you mean? Is he having some kind of work done on his apartment or something?" That would make sense.

Absently rubbing her growing belly, Jillian sighed. "No. He had to go out of town and wasn't sure how long he'd be gone, so he asked us to take care of Rex for him."

Cassie's stomach dropped. It was just like with Tony. She broke the news, and he left town the next day. It was happening all over again. Clutching the table, she felt the little bit of juice she'd managed to get down curdle in her stomach.

"No, Cassie, it isn't like that. He's not running away. He said he had some business to take care of, that's all.

He's coming back." She scooted closer and grabbed Cassie's hand, squeezing it in reassurance. "Listen, you have to be logical. Even if he wasn't in love with you—and I know he is—his job, his apartment and his mom are all here. He's not going to just walk away from all that, right?"

Breathing carefully, Cassie worked to calm herself. Jillian was right. He had to come back. Alex had responsibilities here that he wouldn't abandon in the middle of the night. He had an apartment full of stuff and a job that expected him. Of course, he could be out looking for a new job and a new apartment. Just because he was coming back didn't mean he was planning to stay. "Did he say anything about what he was doing, or where he was going?"

"No, he didn't. He said he couldn't say anything yet. But Cassie, you're going to make yourself crazy if you keep imagining the worst. Alex is a good man, and you know it. You've got to give him some slack, give him a chance to prove himself to you."

Could she do that? Could she put aside her trust issues and hope for the best? Or would she just be setting herself up for even more heartbreak?

Alex's flight landed right on time, setting down on a small runway in what seemed like the middle of the ocean. Grabbing his carry-on bag from the overhead compartment, he made his way off the surprisingly small plane and stood in line at the customs checkpoint. Traveling from Florida to the Bahamas was commonplace, and the whole procedure took only a few minutes. Outside, he entered the first car in a line of waiting taxis and instructed the driver to take him to the Harbor Bay Marina.

His sources had indicated the charter boat Tony was working on operated out of that marina. The charter company's website said it specialized in half-day trips, morning and evening, which meant it should be docked for the next hour or so between sessions. That should be plenty of time to have a one-on-one chat with the deadbeat dad. He didn't want to waste more time on this guy than he had to.

Paying the driver with American dollars wasn't a problem, since Bahamian dollars were pegged to the American dollar, so both were equal in value and accepted everywhere in the small country. Finding the right boat was a bit more difficult. His information didn't include the slip number. He did have the boat's name, though, and hopefully someone would be able to point him in the right direction. Otherwise, he'd have to wander around hoping to find it, and with hundreds of vessels docked in the marina, it could be back out on the open ocean long before he finished his search.

Turning slowly, Alex scanned the marina in an attempt to get his bearings. Five long wooden docks stretched out into the turquoise water where boats of different sizes and shapes were docked. Set back from the water was a cluster of buildings. There was what looked to be a restaurant with indoor and outdoor seating, a store selling tourist-style clothing, and another, smaller shop that looked to be more of a bait and tackle store. He headed for that one, assuming that a fishing charter would at least occasionally need to buy supplies from there.

A buzzing fluorescent bulb and large open windows

lighted the store. Narrow aisles offered a dizzying array of equipment, some of which he knew to be top-of-the-line. Striding toward the back of the store, he noted that it seemed clean and well kept, despite the lingering smell of salt and fish. At the rear counter he found an elderly man with dark, weathered skin and close-cropped silver hair playing solitaire.

"Need some bait?" he asked while slapping down cards.

"No, but I could use some help. I'm looking for a boat, the *Marlin's Lair*. Do you know where I could find it?"

"You looking to charter a trip?"

"Something like that."

The old man's bushy eyebrows narrowed. "Maybe you could explain why you're lookin' and then maybe I can tell you where to look."

Deciding honesty would work better than a lie, Alex nodded. "I'm looking for someone. Do you know a Tony Williams?"

"I do." His tone implied he wasn't happy about the fact.

Sensing an ally, Alex laid it out for him. "He's got a little girl. She's four and has never met him, never gotten any support from him. Her mama seems to think that's for the best, and the look on your face tells me she's right. If that's the case, I'm here to find out if he's willing to keep staying away and put it in writing. If he's not, then I need to know that, too."

The shopkeeper's gaze was sharp and assessing. "I'm thinking the girl and her mama mean something to you, yes?"

Alex swallowed hard. "They mean everything to me."

"I thought so." He smiled and shuffled his cards while he talked. "If Tony's working today, and with that one you never know, he'll be at slip fifty-six. He's blond, kind of skinny, probably looks hungover."

Grateful for the help and the silent vote of confidence, Alex said goodbye and walked back out into the blazing sunlight. Even in mid-February, the temperature was nearing eighty degrees, although the ocean breeze kept it from feeling too warm. Making his way down the seawall, he kept his eyes on the slip numbers. The second long dock held slips fifty to one hundred, and a few spots down he could see a fishing boat matching the description of the *Marlin's Lair*.

Shading his eyes, he watched for signs of anyone on board as he walked down the rough wooden planks toward the boat. No one was in sight, but there was a radio blaring from somewhere below deck. Now what? Go aboard and see what happened, or wait for someone to come out? Time wasn't his friend, but boarding a strange ship unannounced probably wasn't the smartest move.

Movement near the bow of the boat caught his eye. Someone was coming around from the far side, a rag and cleaner in his hands. He was tall and lanky with sun-bleached hair falling in his eyes. He fit the description, but was it Tony? Only one way to tell.

"Tony Williams?"

"Yeah, I'm Tony."

"Mind if I come aboard?" Not waiting for an answer, he stepped onto the deck.

Setting down the rag in his hand, Tony flipped the hair out of his eyes and squinted at Alex. "Do I know you?"

"No, but we do have a mutual acquaintance. I'm a friend of Cassie Marshall's."

Shock and then panic flashed across the man's face. "What the hell? I haven't even talked to her since—"

"Since you found out she was pregnant?" Alex stepped in closer and caught the familiar scent of old booze and desperation. He'd smelled that same ugly combination on his father more times than he could count. Pity mixed with the anger already churning in his gut. The guy had abandoned his daughter, and for what? To drink and party his way into an early grave?

As Tony shuffled backward, his eyes darted back and forth, no doubt looking for an escape route. "What, you looking to run away again? You seem to be pretty good at that. What I want to know is, are you going to stay lost? Or does Cassie need to get her lawyer working on Plan B?"

"Plan B? What the hell is that?"

Alex smiled, his thumbs in his belt loops. "It's where she adds up all the child support you owe, and you start paying it."

"You gotta be kidding me. Listen, I was young. I couldn't take care of a kid—"

"You were older than Cassie, and she still had to do it. Without you. And she'll keep doing it without you, but she's worried you're going to show up one day and decide to play daddy dearest."

"What? What the hell would I do that for? I haven't bothered her yet, have I?"

Bothered? How about hadn't paid child support, helped out, or made any effort to bond with his daughter? "I guess she thought you might want to get to know your daughter at some point."

Tony shook his head. "She doesn't need a guy like me screwing up her life. And I don't have a lot of time, you know, for stuff like that. I'm fine just doing my own thing, and they can do theirs."

"I can see that, but legally, it doesn't work that way."

"What do you mean?"

"What I mean is, in the eyes of the law, you're her father."

"No, man, I'm telling you. I'm not cut out for the father thing, you know?"

"Unless you sign away your rights, it doesn't matter if you're cut out for it or not."

"Wait, I can sign something, and that's it? I don't have to pay anything or do anything?"

"If that's what you want. It would mean you agree you have no more rights as her father. No custody, nothing."

Tony's face blanched. "Custody? I don't even know where I'm going to be staying half the time. I don't want any kind of custody. You tell Cassie to give me the papers and I'll sign them. I just want to be left alone."

Chapter Eighteen

Cassie tucked Emma into her bed, smoothing sheets that would inevitably end up tossed on the floor by the morning. "I was thinking we might go by Grandma and Grandpa's tomorrow after church. Would you like that?"

Emma nodded and snuggled farther down under the covers. "That will be fun."

Fun for Emma. Not so much for Cassie. Having to tell them she was pregnant again wasn't on her top-ten list of ways to have a good time. But it had to be done. Her father was scheduled to come back to work on Monday and it wouldn't take him long to figure it out, considering she couldn't take X-rays while she was pregnant. And she'd need to be a little more careful of lifting, as well. With her dad not fully up to par and both her and Jillian pregnant, things were going to get interesting pretty quickly; in fact, they'd probably have to hire some extra help. Nothing about any of this was going to be simple, but then, nothing ever was.

Except her love for Emma. Leaning down, she pressed a kiss to Emma's forehead, smelling the baby shampoo she still used. "Good night, baby. Sleep tight."

"Night, Mommy," Emma mumbled, her eyes already closed. After spending a good portion of the day at the Sandpiper playing with the dogs, her little girl was worn out. Someday they'd get their own dog, but not now with a baby on the way. Housebreaking a puppy and changing diapers with only a four-year-old to help didn't sound like a very good plan.

Leaving Emma to sleep, she wandered the house, feeling lost. Laundry was piling up in the hampers, the dishwasher was ready to be emptied and there were bills to pay. All the normal things she'd neglected this weekend needed to be done, and she didn't have the energy or motivation for any of it. But avoidance wasn't a valid strategy, not even for housework. Grabbing a basket, she started with the laundry. Her scrubs and Emma's school clothes went into the washer, then the fancy smelling detergent she splurged on. Everyone said the generic stuff worked just as well, but when your job entailed blood and bodily fluids, it was nice to know your clothes smelled pretty.

She'd just closed the lid and turned the machine on when she heard a knock at the door. It was half past eight; who on earth would be stopping by on a Saturday evening? Mollie, maybe; she sometimes came by when she needed help with her college chemistry class. But usually she called first. More curious than concerned, Cassie set the basket on top of the washer and went to look.

More knocking had her gritting her teeth. Whoever

it was, they had better not wake up Emma. She normally was a sound sleeper, but still, there was no need to pound like that. Throwing open the door, she started to say so, and froze. Alex. Now, that was unexpected.

He looked like hell with bloodshot eyes and wrinkled clothes and somehow still made her knees weak. "Can I come in?"

Wordlessly, she let him pass, closing the door behind him. She wanted to go to him. It would feel so good to just lean into him, let him carry some of the worries that weighed her down. Instead she stood her ground, hands on hips, and waited.

"How are you? Are you feeling okay?"

Damn it. Staying strong was hard enough without him being all nice. "I'm fine. I have to admit, I was surprised to see Rex at Jillian's today. I wasn't sure what I was expecting from you after last night, but you leaving town wasn't it. Although, given my limited experience, maybe I should have."

Alex winced as if she'd dealt him a physical blow. "I'm so sorry. I thought I'd be back before you even knew I was gone."

"No, it's fine. You needed some space or something." At least he came back.

Fiddling with the manila envelope in his hands, he took a step toward her. "Actually, I just had something I had to take care of. Something that involves you and Emma." He handed her the envelope. "I had an attorney friend of mine draw these up. I hope that's okay. She's good. I trust her."

An attorney? Was he filing for custody already? She took the paperwork, hating that her hands shook. "Maybe I should just have my lawyer look this over later."

"I'd really like you to read it, please. It's important."

Giving in, she sank onto the couch, tucking her feet up under her. In front of her, Alex paced with the nervous energy of someone who had passed exhaustion hours ago. Whatever this was, he seemed to have put a heck of a lot of effort into getting it. Unfastening the little metal clasp, she slid out the stack of papers inside. Most of it was a jumble of legalese, but the purpose of the forms was clear. At the top, printed in bold letters, were the words Petition for Termination of Parental Rights. Tears blurred her vision, obscuring the rest of the document, not that she needed to see more. He was abandoning this baby, just like her ex had abandoned Emma. With more class, maybe, but in the end, the result was the same.

"You didn't waste much time, did you?"

"When something needs to be done, I do it. I thought you'd be grateful to have things wrapped up, finally."

Finally? It had been only one day. He'd found out she was pregnant and found a lawyer to write up papers to rid himself of the problem in one day. And on a weekend, no less. He couldn't even wait until Monday, when the offices would be open. No, he went God knows where to track down someone who could do it on a Saturday. So much for giving him the benefit of the doubt or thinking he was too responsible to walk out on his own child. She should have been listening to his words, not her heart. He'd told her he wasn't ready to be a father and now he wanted to put it in writing.

Shoving up from the couch, she threw the papers down, resisting the petty urge to stomp on them. "You can take your damn papers, Alex. I'm not signing anything."

* * *

"What?" Alex stood amid the papers scattered on the floor and tried to figure out when the woman he loved had completely lost her mind. Her face was flushed with anger and if looks could kill, he'd need his Kevlar vest. Was she upset that he'd gotten involved in her private life? Or had she been wanting her ex to come back, after all? "I thought this was what you wanted."

Her eyes grew wider as she stared at him, tears streaming down her face. "What? Why would you think I wanted this?"

"Well, when we talked about Emma and her father, you said you worried he'd come back one day—"

"So you decided to make sure I never had to worry about that with you?" She stomped off to the kitchen and he followed at a cautious distance. Knives were in the kitchen, after all. She'd filled the kettle and set it on the stove before her words penetrated his brain.

"Wait, what? What do you mean, worry about it with me? What does this have to do with us?"

She slammed her mug down so hard, he half expected it to crack in her hand. "Signing away your rights to this baby has everything to do with us. How on earth can you think otherwise?"

His rights? "I'm not signing anything away."

Exasperated, she pointed back at the living room. "Then why did you get the papers drawn up? Are you just messing with me? Because it's not funny."

His sleep-deprived brain finally started to make the connection. "You think the papers are about our baby?"

"Who else would they be for?"

Rounding the counter, he put his hands on her shoulders, steadying her. "Tony signed those, not me.

I tracked him down, and he's willing to give up his rights, permanently."

Cassie went boneless under his hands, nearly collapsing. Propping her up, he led her to a stool at the counter before letting her go to turn off the now-screeching kettle.

"You found Tony? When? How?" Blinking rapidly, she stared at him. "And more than that, why? Why would you do that?"

"One thing at a time." He poured the water into her mug and added a tea bag from the canister on the counter. Pushing it toward her, he sat down on the other stool. "I started looking for him a little while ago. I have some contacts down south, private investigators and such, and I thought they might be able to track him down. And I talked to a woman I know from the district attorney's office in Miami. She works for a private practice now and has a reputation for protecting kids. I wanted to find out what the options were—she's the one who drew up the legal forms. When you told me you were pregnant I decided to push forward."

Emma swallowed hard. "Don't you think you should have discussed this with me first?"

"Maybe. Probably. But at first I didn't know where he was. And then, last night—well, you weren't in the mood to discuss things. Besides, I didn't want to get your hopes up if I couldn't find him. But I did find him, working on a boat in the Bahamas. He's been there ever since he left, probably afraid that if he came back to the States, you'd make him pay child support."

"So that's where you were today? You flew to the Bahamas?"

He nodded.

She rubbed at her eyes, exhaustion showing on her face. She didn't look as if she'd slept much more than he had. "We can talk about it tomorrow," he said, "if you're too tired—"

"No. I want to know the whole story. What did you say to him? What did he say? What does he want?"

"I told him I knew you and his daughter, and you deserved to know if he was coming back. I also reminded him that he owed quite a bit of child support. As for what he wants, he just wants to be left alone. He has no interest in custody or anything else and said to tell you he'd sign whatever he has to sign."

"So that's it? He signed the papers and he's out of our lives for good?"

"Basically, yeah. I mean, the judge has to approve it, but given the circumstances it shouldn't be a problem."

"I know I should say thank you, but I can't even wrap my head around this yet. And the dumb thing is, part of me is sad. Not because I want to see him," she added quickly. "But it sucks that he couldn't pull it together enough to be there for her, that he doesn't even want to know her or anything."

"That's not dumb at all. It is sad, but from where I sit, he's the one missing out." He placed his hand on hers, stroking her soft skin with this thumb. "No man in his right mind could walk away from you and Emma."

Cassie's pulse pounded in her ears. Was he trying to say he wasn't going to walk away? This was way too much information way too fast, and she couldn't think straight with him touching her. Pulling her hand away, she stood up and headed for the patio. Maybe some fresh air would help her clear her mind so she could make sense of everything.

Behind her, she heard Alex let out a low whistle as he stepped outside. "This is amazing."

Smiling, she sat down on her favorite chair. "It is pretty wonderful, isn't it?"

"It's like something out of a magazine. You could charge admission."

She gave a mock shudder at the thought. "I don't think so. This is where I come to get away from everything. No tourists allowed."

"Well, then, I'm honored to be allowed into the inner sanctuary."

"You should be," she said with a grin. It was crazy how easy he was to be around. After all the stress of the day and the shock of his news, she should have been a basket case. But being near him somehow helped put her mind at ease. Which *was* crazy, considering most of her stress could be traced back to him.

"Are you okay? I know this was what you wanted, but like you said, it's still a big deal."

"I'll be okay. But I have to know. What made you decide to get involved? Why go to all this trouble?"

He pulled a chair over, the metal legs scraping across the concrete. As he sat down, his brown eyes shone with an intensity she hadn't seen before. "I didn't decide to get involved. I already am involved. Up to my eyebrows. But I knew you couldn't move forward—we couldn't move forward—if you were constantly looking over your shoulder, waiting for your past to show up and ruin things. I wanted to give us a fresh start."

"Us?"

He leaned closer, taking both of her hands in his.

"Yes, us. You, me, Emma…and the baby. Our baby. Whatever happens, I'm not running away. I'm not your ex, and I'm not my father."

"But…" Her brain stuttered and stalled. "I thought you didn't want children. You said you were scared—"

"I am scared. Hell, I'm terrified." He grinned and squeezed her hands. "But just because something is scary doesn't mean I'm going to turn tail and run. I've faced down drug dealers and gang bangers. I think I can handle an unarmed baby."

"Really?"

"Really. I admit the idea of being a father frightens me. But you know what frightens me more?"

She shook her head, emotion a lump in her throat.

"Losing my chance with you."

"You still want to be with me?" Maybe she'd heard wrong, misunderstood. She'd been doing a lot of that lately.

"If you'll have me." His voice was rough but sensual, like the ocean during a storm. Goose bumps dotted her arms as if he was already touching her.

"You're sure?" she whispered, afraid of breaking the spell if she spoke too loudly or moved too quickly.

Alex's words, on the other hand, were loud and clear. "I've never been more sure of anything in my life." He drew her into his lap, settling her against the hard planes of his body. "I'm not saying it's going to be easy. I don't know how it's all going to work, but I know that I want to try."

Curling into him, she let herself feel all the things she'd been denying. He was there, he wasn't leaving and he felt so very good pressed against her in the dark. Turning her head toward him, she looked for something in his eyes to tell her this was a mistake. But all she saw were sincerity, trust and a longing that matched her own. He'd made no promises for the future, but his pledge to try meant more than any declaration of love could. Honesty was what she needed, not pretty words.

"Would it be okay if I kiss you now? I've been dying to since our dance last night." His breath tickled her ear as he spoke, sending little sparks up and down her spine.

In answer, she reached up and brought his lips down hard on hers, kissing him with all the pent-up fear and hope and worry and love that had tangled her up in knots. He met her intensity with his own heat and passion. Everything she didn't know how to say, she said with her lips against his, her body molding against him. Only when she was afraid she might actually explode with need did she pull away, panting in his arms.

"Wow." His eyes had gone nearly black under the starlight, and she could feel his heart pounding through his chest. "If leaving town for the day results in that kind of treatment, I'm going to be gone a whole lot."

She smacked him on the arm. "Not funny."

He winced. "I suppose not. Chalk it up to my lack of sleep. I'm running on empty, and as good as that kiss was, I should get myself home before I'm too tired to drive."

He was leaving already? She'd pictured something much more...well...intimate happening. "You could stay."

"I can't. I called Nic when I landed and told him I'd be by soon to pick up Rex. Besides, there's Emma. I don't want our first conversation about us to be when she wakes up and finds me in your bed. That's not fair to her."

She sighed. "You're right. I don't want that, either. You just make me so crazy, I can't think straight."

"Good." He kissed the tip of her nose. "I love that you're just as affected as I am. Now, you're going to have to get out of my lap or I'm never going to be able to make myself go."

Sliding out of his lap, she could feel exactly how much he wanted to stay. "When will I see you again?"

"Is tomorrow soon enough?"

Alex watched Cassie's face turn serious. "Actually, we have plans tomorrow."

"Oh." Maybe he'd read her wrong and she was still mad?

"No, don't be upset. I do want to see you, but we are going to my parents' house tomorrow after church." She laid a hand on her still-flat belly. "I need to tell them about the baby."

"Tomorrow?" Heck, he'd just found out himself; he'd thought he would have a little time to get used to the idea before they started telling people. Not that he was ashamed, but he would have liked to have a plan, and ideally a ring, before that news got out.

Cassie grimaced. "I know. I'm not wild about everyone finding out, either. But my dad's coming back to work on Monday, and I won't be able to hide it. There are safety issues, with radiation and anesthesia and such."

He hadn't even thought of that. He'd been so wrapped up in his own baggage, he hadn't even considered how she would juggle the pregnancy with her career. "Is it safe for you to keep working? Because if it's about the money, I can—"

"Don't worry. I'll be safe. I just have to take a few extra precautions. Which means I have to tell my dad now, and he can't keep a secret from my mom to save his life, so I might as well tell both of them at once. I'm not exactly looking forward to it, but it is what it is. They need to know. Might as well get it over with."

"Then I'll go with you." This was as much his doing as hers, and if she was brave enough to face her parents, the least he could do was be there to support her.

"What? No, you don't have to do that."

"I know I don't have to, but I want to. I should be there for you. And your parents need to know that I'm going to be a part of this baby's life, and yours, if you let me. After Tony, I think I may have my work cut out for me."

She grinned. "They already love you. After you found Emma...trust me, liking you isn't a problem. I'm the one that they'll be disappointed in. Again."

"You've got to be kidding me. How could anyone be disappointed in you? You've raised an amazing little girl on your own and made an impressive career for yourself. I can't imagine they are anything but impressed by you."

Shadows clouded her eyes, but she nodded. "Maybe. We'll see, I guess. But are you sure you want to do this?"

Did he want to? Not exactly. But she needed to do this, so he needed to be there. They were a team now, whether she realized it or not. "I'll be there. Just tell me when and where."

"We'll go after the ten o'clock service, if that's all right. Emma doesn't want to miss Sunday school."

"I'll be there. I already arranged to have the rest of the weekend off."

"Well, okay, then." She looked at the door, then at him, as if trying to find another reason for him to stay. A feeling he shared, but couldn't give in to. But if he had his way, there wouldn't be too many more late-night goodbyes.

"Good night, Cassie." He gave her a soft, lingering kiss that only reminded him how much he wanted to stay. Still tasting her, he pressed a hand to her belly. "Good night, baby. Don't give your mama too hard a time, okay?"

Cassie bit her lip, tears shining in her eyes. He hated that she was so surprised by the smallest bit of affection from him. Knowing how hurt she'd been made him want to go right back to the Bahamas and feed Tony to the sharks. Giving her one last quick kiss on the forehead, he let himself out while he still could.

Outside the stars were shining as if they'd been polished, each a bright pinprick of light against the dark island sky. Getting in the truck, he wondered again at the circumstances that had brought him here. If his partner hadn't screwed up, if he and his fellow officers hadn't betrayed him, if the Palmetto County sheriff's office hadn't had an opening at just the right time, he might never have come to Paradise, never met Cassie or Emma. Now, driving through the quiet streets on the way to pick up his dog, he couldn't imagine living anywhere else.

Paradise had given him a place to lick his wounds, to start over. But the island was more than a temporary sanctuary; it had become a real home. Maybe part of that was meeting Cassie; it was hard to say. Both the woman and the place had seduced him, and he had no intentions of letting go of either one.

At the Sandpiper, he walked quietly up the stairs and through the front door. The front desk was vacant, but lying in front of the fireplace in the main lobby were Rex and Murphy, both passed out. In a similar state, Nic was sprawled on one of the loveseats, eyes closed and an open book on his chest. The dogs noticed Alex first. Rex stretched like a cat, then rolled over for a belly rub. "Wow, I'm gone all day and you don't even bother to get up and say hello?"

A rumble from the couch drew his attention back to Nic, who was now sitting up and rubbing his eyes. "So, how did it go? Did you find him?"

"I did. I even got a bit of help from a local. It seems he's not very well liked down there."

"Imagine that." Nic stood and stretched. "So, what did he say?"

"He signed away his rights. He'd do anything to avoid paying all the child support he owes. You know, he didn't even ask about Emma. Didn't want to know how she's doing or see a picture. Nothing." At least Alex's old man had tried. He'd cared, but it just hadn't been enough. "If nothing else, I can understand now why Cassie was so sure Emma was better off without him."

Nic nodded and walked to the kitchen, snagging a couple of sodas from the fridge and handing one to Alex. "How did Cassie take the news?"

"Not well at first. She saw the papers and thought I was giving up my rights to our baby."

"Oh, wow. Way to mess that up."

"No kidding. But once I explained, everything was

fine. Better than fine." He smiled, thinking of that amazing kiss on the patio.

"Hot damn, good for you. So, when's the wedding?"

Alex coughed, spewing soda down the front of his shirt. Nic laughed and handed him a towel.

"Don't tell me you haven't thought about it. Remember, I proposed to Jillian not long ago, so I know the signs."

No point in pretending. "Fine, yes, I'm thinking about it. But I don't know if she's ready yet. I want things to be right."

"Dude, she's in love with you and she's pregnant with your child. What else are you waiting for?"

Chapter Nineteen

Nic's words haunted him. Tossing and turning all night, he asked himself this: What was he waiting for? He loved her. He was certain of that. And he wanted them to be a family. Fatherhood hadn't been the plan, but if he was going to do it, he wanted to do it right. Part-time wasn't enough, not after all the time he'd missed out on with his own father. He wanted to be there when Cassie felt the first kicks, to rub her feet when they hurt or buy her ice cream when she craved it. And most of all, he wanted to make love to her every night and wake up to her soft body against his each morning.

Which was why he was up and knocking on his mother's door at what felt like the break of dawn. Scratching at his two-day beard, he waited for the door to open. Hopefully he'd caught her before she left for Mass.

"Alex?" His mother's worried face appeared at the open door. "What are you doing here so early? Is everything okay?"

"It's fine, Mama. I just needed to talk to you about something."

Relaxing, she accepted a hug and shooed him toward the kitchen. "There's coffee ready, and I'll make us some breakfast while you tell me what's so important."

"Just coffee, please. I'm not hungry."

She pinned him with a hard stare. "Not hungry? Are you sick?"

"No, Mama, I'm not sick. I'm fine, in fact. I promise."

She scrutinized him as if looking for some sign of illness before turning away to pour the coffee. "This is about your animal-doctor friend, then, yes?"

How did she always know? He accepted the cup of strong, rich coffee and took a sip, waiting for her to sit at the table with him. Instead, she stood over him, watching with the same sharp gaze that had intimidated him as a child. This time, however, he wasn't confessing some childish sin.

"So? What is it that has you so tied up in knots you can't even eat your mama's cooking? Did you mess things up with her? Because if you did, you need to face up to it and make it right."

There was no way to say this, other than just to say it. "She's pregnant, Mama."

His mother narrowed her lips, considering. "And are you the father?"

"Yes, ma'am." He was in for it now; he'd sat through enough lectures as a teenager to know her feelings about premarital sex and unintended pregnancies.

"Oh, Alex." Tears filled her eyes as she smiled. "A baby? I'm going to be a grandmother?"

Stunned, he nodded as she fanned her eyes. Wasn't she supposed to be yelling at him? "I thought you'd be upset. Because of what the Church says and—"

"The Church says babies are a blessing. And that's what this baby will be. Anything else is water under the bridge."

The knotted muscles in his shoulders released a bit. He hadn't quite realized how worried he'd been about her reaction until now. "Thank you for being so supportive. It means a lot."

She smacked his shoulder, tears still slipping down her face. "Don't be silly. I'm your mama. Now, are you ready for breakfast, or is there more?"

"Well, there is one other thing." He grinned. "I wanted to ask about Grandma's ring. I'm going to ask Cassie to marry me."

His mother wrapped her arms around him, nearly smothering him in her enthusiasm. "Mom, you're choking me."

She gave a final squeeze, then stood up, smiling as if he'd won the Nobel Prize and the World Series all on the same day. "A wedding and a baby. The ladies at the senior center are going to be so jealous."

"You're going to have to hold off on bragging for now. She hasn't said yes yet. And she doesn't want to tell people about the pregnancy right away, I don't think. We haven't even told her parents yet. I'm meeting her over there for lunch."

Her face fell a bit, but she nodded. "Then I'll wait. Oh, let me go get you the ring."

He finished his coffee while she rummaged in her

bedroom. Who'd have thought his strict, super-religious mother would have reacted so well? He knew he was doing the right thing, but it was nice to know he had her support.

"Here you are. Your grandfather gave it to your grandmother, and she gave it to me. Now you will give it to Cassie." She placed the small plain box on the table in front of him. Opening it, he found the ring as he remembered it—a brilliant round diamond resting in an antique setting. Hand-wrought scrollwork covered the elegant platinum band, and inside was inscribed the word *Forever*. He could buy a new ring, but somehow he thought Cassie would appreciate the significance of a family heirloom.

"Thank you. It's beautiful. She has to say yes now."

"She'll say yes because she loves you. I was trying not to pry, but I saw you at the Sandpiper the other night on the dance floor. She looked at you the way a woman looks at the man she loves."

"I hope so." He didn't know what he'd do if she said no. Which was why he wasn't going to ask until he'd had time to prove himself to her. He couldn't risk rushing her and pushing her away.

"Remember, don't say anything. We'll tell her parents today about the baby, but then she needs some time. I'm not going to rush her, so you're just going to have to be patient."

"I won't say a thing. Now go get cleaned up before you go over there. You look like something the cat dragged in."

"Gee, thanks." Between her and Nic, his ego was taking a beating. "You sure know how to flatter a guy."

She waved her finger at him. "You don't need flattery. You need a shower and a shave. Maybe a haircut, too. I can get my scissors—"

"No, no, that's okay. I'll take care of it." He put the ring in his pocket and gave her a hug goodbye. He was grateful for her support, but right now the woman he needed to see was Cassie.

Cassie bowed her head for the closing prayer, adding her "Amen" to those of the congregation. Once the organ belted out the final hymn, she made her way up the aisle to the main doors, dodging the line of people waiting to shake hands with the priest. Normally she would join the throngs that stood around chatting after the service, but today she was too keyed up.

Emma was just finishing up her snack when Cassie got to her classroom to pick her up. Her craft for the week, an angel with glittery wings, was drying on the table next to her. "Hey, sweetie, time to go to Grandma and Grandpa's house."

Emma sucked the last of her juice from the little cardboard box and nodded. After saying her goodbyes she walked out with Cassie, clutching her masterpiece, as if it were made of jewels instead of glue and glitter. "Can I give my angel to Grandma?"

"Sure, honey. I bet she'd like that." Loading her into the car seat, Cassie was careful not touch the glue on Emma's still-wet creation. "Oh, and Deputy Alex is going to be there, too. Is that okay?"

The little girl's eyes lit up. "Yay! Is he going to bring Rex, too?"

"I don't know. Maybe." Starting the car, she headed toward her parents' home on the outskirts of town. But-terflies flew a serpentine pattern in her stomach as she got closer, a combination of nerves, anticipation and hormones. Rolling her window down helped. The rush of fresh salt air settled her stomach and cleared her head, leaving just the excitement of seeing Alex again. She needed to know that what happened last night wasn't a dream. It had seemed real last night, but in the light of day it was hard to believe.

Turning into the driveway, she spotted Alex's SUV parked by the house. He was early—maybe he was as eager to see her as she was to see him. Pulse thrumming, she let Emma out of the car and headed up the walk. They were still a few feet from the house when a loud bark announced their presence.

"Rex is here!" Emma broke into a run, her paper project fluttering in her hand.

"Hey, there." Alex opened the front door and watched Emma fly by him to look for her furry friend. "I guess I know which of us she really wanted to see." He smiled at Cassie, his dimples doing dangerous things to her heart.

"Sorry. Don't take it personally."

"I won't." He leaned down and gave her a quick kiss, then took hold of her hand. "I missed you."

Her cheeks heated. "I missed you, too. I was afraid I'd dreamed last night."

He lowered his voice so only she could hear. "Honey, if last night had been a dream, it would have ended with us in bed, not with me leaving to pick up my dog."

Every nerve ending flared. How was she going to get through today with that thought tormenting her?

"Cassie, there you are. Come on back. Alex was helping me man the grill."

Startled, she tried to drop Alex's hand, but he kept a firm grip.

"I don't want to hide, Cassie. Especially given the circumstances. Unless you have some reason you don't want people to know about us?"

"No, it's not that. I'm just…surprised, I guess. I'm not used to thinking of us as, well, an *us*." He'd said he wanted to make things work, to be with her, but what did that mean, really? One minute she was rude to him, the next he saved her daughter, and now they were having a kid together. Where in all of that did holding hands fit in?

Apparently not as prone to overthinking as she was, Alex pulled her along with him to the back patio. At the far end, sweet-smelling smoke wafted from the grill. Down on the grass, Emma was playing some kind of elaborate game with Rex involving a half dozen tennis balls and a soccer net.

Her father turned from cooking the food when they came out, his eyes widening a fraction when he saw them holding hands. Looking from one to the other, he raised an eyebrow. "Elizabeth, why don't you come out here and join us?"

Her mother stepped out onto the patio, wearing a striped apron over her jeans and blouse. "What is it, David? I'm not done with the coleslaw yet."

He reached into his wallet and pulled out a ten-dollar bill. "I just wanted to pay up on our little bet."

"Bet?" Cassie glared at her father. "What bet?"

Her mother took the money and tucked it into her apron pocket. "Your father was being hardheaded and wouldn't listen when I told him you two were falling for each other." She shrugged. "Anyone could see it."

Cassie's mouth dropped open. They'd bet on her love life?

"Sorry I cost you a bet, sir," Alex said with a grin.

"No worries. You making my daughter happy is worth more than all the money in the world. Just take good care of her."

Alex cleared his throat and squared his shoulders. "I fully intend to, sir. Her and the baby."

"Excuse me?" Her father's shocked tone matched the look on her mother's face. "Baby?"

Stepping forward, Cassie met his gaze head-on. "I'm pregnant, Daddy. I'm sorry."

"Sorry. What do you mean, sorry?" Her mother waved away the apology. "You've always said you wanted a sibling for Emma someday. And we've always wanted more grandchildren, haven't we, David?"

At her mother's heated look, he quickly capitulated. "Of course we have. I was just surprised a bit, that's all. You two haven't known each other that long and—"

"And nothing, David Andrew Marshall. Love has its own timing, doesn't it, honey?" She held out her arms and Cassie accepted the hug, her eyes filling. "Now, when is this little bundle of joy going to make an appearance? We have so much to plan—a baby shower, your registry—"

"A wedding," Alex said.

"What did you say?" Cassie asked. She couldn't have heard that right. Except her parents looked as stunned as she felt.

"A wedding." He moved directly in front of Cassie, his gaze never wavering from hers. "I was planning to ask you later, when things calmed down." He shrugged. "It kind of slipped out."

"It slipped out? What on earth is that supposed to

mean?" She heard the hysteria in her voice, but didn't particularly care. What did he expect with an announcement like that?

He ran a hand through his hair and took a deep breath. "It means that I messed up and got everything out of order, again." He turned to Cassie's father. "Sir, I'd planned to talk to you and Mrs. Marshall and ask for your blessing. Heck, I wanted to talk to Emma, too, and feel her out on the idea."

"And when was all this supposed to happen?" Cassie asked. Everything was happening so fast. Just last night she'd thought he was running out on her; now he wanted to marry her?

"Not for a while. I thought you needed some time to adjust to the idea of us being together, to learn to trust me."

"I do trust you. I know I haven't acted like it, but I do."

"Well, then, maybe it's better this way. I know it's fast, but Cassie, I don't want to wait. I know what I want, and I want you."

Dumbfounded, she watched him pull a small box out of his pocket and get down on one knee.

Behind him, Emma climbed up the steps to come lean against Cassie's side. "What's he doing, Mommy? Did he fall down?"

Alex smiled at her. "I did fall, for you and your mommy. In fact, I'm head over heels in love with both of you."

Emma tilted her head, looking for injuries. "Are you going to be okay?"

"Well, that depends."

Heart thumping wildly, Cassie let him take her hand.

Everything was happening in slow motion; even the birds seemed to have stopped chirping. "Cassie Marshall, you've already filled my heart and changed my life. I don't want to ever give that up. Please, will you marry me?"

"Mommy, say yes," Emma said in a stage whisper, her eyes like saucers.

Cassie hugged the little girl and whispered back, "I don't know. You think he might make an okay daddy?"

Emma nodded. "The best, and he'll bring Rex, too!"

Laughing, Cassie looked back down at Alex. "In that case, yes, Alex Santiago, I'll marry you." She winked at Emma. "But you have to bring Rex with you."

Chapter Twenty

Cassie pulled the last pin from her hair and breathed a sigh of relief. The fancy updo her mother had talked her into had turned out gorgeous, but she felt more herself with her curls loose around her shoulders. Across the room, Alex watched, his eyes smoky with desire. Sprawled on the bed, his bow tie long gone and his tuxedo shirt open at the neck, he was the sexiest man she'd ever seen. And as of a few hours ago, he was her husband.

She'd wanted a small, quiet ceremony, but between her mother and Alex's mom, who was possibly the sweetest woman on the planet, she'd been outvoted. Almost half the island had ended up in attendance. At least she'd gotten her way with the location. They'd been married in her parents' backyard, only a month after Alex had proposed. Tomorrow, they'd be leaving for their honeymoon, a trip to Puerto Rico to meet some of Alex's relatives. But tonight Emma was with her grandparents, and she and Alex were finally alone.

"Think you could help me take off my dress?"

"I thought you'd never ask." In an instant, he was behind her. But before he had a single button undone, there was a knock at the door.

"Don't answer it."

"I have to. It could be my mom—something could be wrong with Emma. I'll be right back, I promise." She started for the front door, the silken skirt of her dress swishing as she walked.

Alex followed, padding barefoot down the hall. "Whoever it is, they had better be quick."

Silently agreeing, Cassie opened the door, then nearly slammed it shut again. Heart pounding, she stared at the man on the doorstep.

Behind her, Alex stiffened. "Who is it?"

Cassie opened the door the rest of the way, making room for Alex to stand beside her. "Jack Campbell, the man I told you about from the accident." Her voice shook, but she stood tall. She was not going to let him frighten her.

Alex stepped forward, positioning himself in front of Cassie. "You shouldn't be here, Jack."

Swallowing, Jack nodded, taking in Cassie's wedding dress and Alex's tux. "I'm sorry, I didn't realize... Well, I mean, I'd heard Dr. Marshall was getting married, but I didn't know it was today."

"Well, it was, and you're interrupting our wedding night. So if you would just go—"

"I will. I just need to say something to the doc first."

He peered around Alex to make eye contact with Cassie. "I just wanted to tell you I'm sorry—"

"Jack, I don't think now is the time—" Alex moved to close the door.

"No, it's okay." She'd spent too long thinking about this; she didn't want to bring it into her new life with Alex. "Let him have his say." Maybe then she could put it behind her.

Jack twisted his hands together. "I came to say I'm sorry about the accident. I'd been drinking that night. Hell, I drank every night. But I'm not drinking anymore—I'm in a program now. One of those twelve-step programs. And one of the steps is to admit my mistakes and try to make things right where I can. I admitted everything to the department, and they put me on a leave of absence." His voice cracked and his shoulders started to shake. "I can't fix what happened to you and your dad, but I'm going to make sure I don't hurt anyone else. I promise you that."

Cassie listened, waiting for the familiar surge of anger she felt whenever she even thought of Jack Campbell. She'd spent months convincing herself she hated him. Here he was, and all she felt was pity. "Thank you, Jack. That means a lot to me."

Alex wrapped an arm around her in support. "Stick with it, man. You have a family that needs you."

"I know, and I'm going to do right by them. Anyway, I'll leave you folks alone now. Oh, and congratulations." Backing down the walk, he grabbed an old bicycle and hopped on. Watching him ride off, she felt free. His confession had given her permission to move on.

"Are you okay?" Alex closed the door, checking that it was locked securely.

"I'm better than okay." She pressed her body against his, feeling the hard muscles of his chest against her breasts. "Now, are you going to make this marriage official or what?"

She barely had the words out before Alex stilled her lips with a kiss. Hungry for her, he teased at her lips, needing to taste her. She moaned into his mouth, pulling at his clothes. Without ending the kiss, he stripped his clothes off, giving her busy hands access to his body. Gritting his teeth against the throbbing need to take her, he pulled back.

"Let me undress you." Slowly, one by one, he undid the long line of pearl buttons, teasing himself with each peek at the skin beneath. As the last one gave way, the dress slid to the floor in a puddle of silk and lace. Dear Lord, she was completely nude underneath. "If I'd known you weren't wearing anything under this, I don't think I would have made it through the ceremony."

She turned, smiling, and his heart skipped a beat. This beautiful, sexy woman was his wife. The soft swell of her belly was his child. "Cassie…"

She came to him, pulling his head down to hers for a soft but sensual kiss. He couldn't wait any longer; she felt too good and he needed her too badly. Sweeping her up into his arms, he carried her down the hall to her bed—their bed now. Afraid of hurting her or the baby, he eased her down on top of him, letting her take control. The first time they'd made love, it had been frantic and out of control. This time, there was no rush, no fumbling, just her body and his, skin to skin and soul to soul until they melted together in a single moment of pure pleasure.

* * *

Near midnight, after yet another round of lovemaking, Cassie collapsed against Alex, loving the way her body fit perfectly against his. Tracing her fingers through his chest hair, she decided now was as good a time as any to ask the question that had been in the back of her mind ever since he proposed. "Alex?"

"Again?" he mumbled, half asleep.

"No. I mean, not now." She sat up, letting the covers fall away. "I wanted to ask you something important."

Rousing himself, he propped himself up on the pillows. "What is it?"

"There's something I've been wondering, and I haven't known how to bring it up."

"Just say it. You can ask me anything."

She took a deep breath, not wanting to spoil the mood but needing to know. "What would you say to the idea of adopting Emma? It wouldn't have to be now, but maybe you'd consider it? She's always wanted a father, and with the baby coming—"

Alex put a finger on her lips, silencing her. "I'd say that, as long as Emma wants me, too, I'd like nothing better. And that I already have an appointment scheduled with my lawyer for the day after we get back from our honeymoon."

Tears filled her eyes. "Have I told you lately what a good husband you are?"

He grinned and pulled her back down on top of him. "No, but I can think of a really fun way for you to show me."

* * * * *

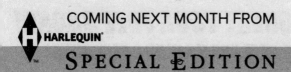

REQUEST YOUR FREE BOOKS!
2 FREE NOVELS PLUS 2 FREE GIFTS!

Ⓗ HARLEQUIN®

SPECIAL EDITION
Life, Love & Family

YES! Please send me 2 FREE Harlequin® Special Edition novels and my 2 FREE gifts (gifts are worth about $10). After receiving them, if I don't wish to receive any more books, I can return the shipping statement marked "cancel." If I don't cancel, I will receive 6 brand-new novels every month and be billed just $4.74 per book in the U.S. or $5.49 per book in Canada. That's a savings of at least 12% off the cover price! It's quite a bargain! Shipping and handling is just 50¢ per book in the U.S. and 75¢ per book in Canada.* I understand that accepting the 2 free books and gifts places me under no obligation to buy anything. I can always return a shipment and cancel at any time. Even if I never buy another book, the two free books and gifts are mine to keep forever.

235/335 HDN GH3Z

Name	(PLEASE PRINT)

Address	Apt. #

City	State/Prov.	Zip/Postal Code

Signature (if under 18, a parent or guardian must sign)

Mail to the **Reader Service:**
IN U.S.A.: P.O. Box 1867, Buffalo, NY 14240-1867
IN CANADA: P.O. Box 609, Fort Erie, Ontario L2A 5X3

Want to try two free books from another line?
Call 1-800-873-8635 or visit www.ReaderService.com.

* Terms and prices subject to change without notice. Prices do not include applicable taxes. Sales tax applicable in N.Y. Canadian residents will be charged applicable taxes. Offer not valid in Quebec. This offer is limited to one order per household. Not valid for current subscribers to Harlequin Special Edition books. All orders subject to credit approval. Credit or debit balances in a customer's account(s) may be offset by any other outstanding balance owed by or to the customer. Please allow 4 to 6 weeks for delivery. Offer available while quantities last.

Your Privacy—The Reader Service is committed to protecting your privacy. Our Privacy Policy is available online at www.ReaderService.com or upon request from the Reader Service.

We make a portion of our mailing list available to reputable third parties that offer products we believe may interest you. If you prefer that we not exchange your name with third parties, or if you wish to clarify or modify your communication preferences, please visit us at www.ReaderService.com/consumerschoice or write to us at Reader Service Preference Service, P.O. Box 9062, Buffalo, NY 14240-9062. Include your complete name and address.

HSE15

Travis had heard the words come out of his mouth and
been as stunned as the two men he'd come to know so well
in recent weeks. Yet as soon as his brain had processed
the audio signals, he'd recognized their unshakable truth.
If trading his Air Force flight suit for one with an EAS
patch on it would win Kate back, he'd make the change
today.

"So what do you think?" he asked her. "Again, your
first no-frills, no-holds-barred gut reaction?"

"I won't lie," she admitted slowly, reluctantly. "My
head, my heart, my gut all leaped for joy."

He started for her, elation pumping through his veins.
The hand she slapped against his chest to stop him made
only a tiny dent in his fierce joy.

"Wait, Trav! This is too big a decision to make without talking it over. Let's…let's use this time together to make sure it's what you really want."

"I'm sure. Now."

"Well, I'm not." Her brown eyes showed an agony of doubt. "The military's been your whole life up to now."

"Wrong." He laid his hand over hers, felt the warmth of her palm against his sternum. "You came first, Katydid. Before the uniform, before the wings, before the head rush and stomach-twisting responsibilities of being part of a crew. I let those get in the way the past few years. That won't happen again."

The doubt was still there in her eyes, swimming in a pool of indecision. He needed to back off, Travis conceded. Give her a few days to accept what was now a done deal in his mind.

"Okay," he said with a sense of rightness he hadn't felt in longer than he could remember, "we'll head up to Venice. Let Ellis's proposal percolate for a day or two."

And then, he vowed, they would conduct a virtual burning of the divorce decree before he took his wife to bed.

Don't miss
"I DO"…TAKE TWO!
by USA TODAY *bestselling author Merline Lovelace,*
available March 2016 wherever
Harlequin® Special Edition books and ebooks are sold.

www.Harlequin.com

Love the Harlequin book you just read?

Your opinion matters.

Review this book on your favorite book site, review site, blog or your own social media properties and share your opinion with other readers!

HARLEQUIN®

A *Romance* FOR EVERY MOOD™

JUST CAN'T GET ENOUGH?

Join our social communities
and talk to us online.

You will have access to the latest
news on upcoming titles and special
promotions, but most importantly,
you can talk to other fans about your
favorite Harlequin reads.

Harlequin.com/Community

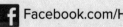 Facebook.com/HarlequinBooks

Twitter.com/HarlequinBooks

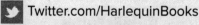 Pinterest.com/HarlequinBooks

THE WORLD IS BETTER WITH

Romance

Harlequin has everything from contemporary, passionate and heartwarming to suspenseful and inspirational stories.

Whatever your mood, we have a romance just for you!

Connect with us to find your next great read, special offers and more.

f /HarlequinBooks

y @HarlequinBooks

www.HarlequinBlog.com

www.Harlequin.com/Newsletters

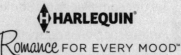

HARLEQUIN®

A *Romance* FOR EVERY MOOD™

www.Harlequin.com